'There is something rich and genuinely strange at the heart of Lanny ... Porter's nature writing has a shamanic intensity to it ... incantatory and alive.' *Literary Review*

'Remarkable for its simultaneous sparseness and extravagance, and ... a book full of love ... Porter's writing is poetically concentrated while also deploying a wonderfully common-or-garden kind of language, loved and used, rolling off the tongue.' *Guardian*

'A Max Porter novel. So you are assured it's like no other. Slim in page count but abundant in magical storytelling.' Sarah Jessica Parker

'A magically beguiling work, a triumph of artistic vision.' *Financial Times*

'An absorbing, evocative tale that manages to be deeply poetic, moving and gripping all at once.' *Daily Record*

'Absorbing, pacy and fresh, and whatever your preconceptions are of English village life, this will give you a new perspective.' *Evening Standard*

'Wonderful ... Porter's prose is mesmerising. It's lyrical, enchanting and terrifying ... A brilliantly claustrophobic read.' Charlotte Heathcote, *Sunday Express*

MAX PORTER

LANNY

FABER & FABER

First published in 2019
by Faber & Faber Limited
Bloomsbury House
74–77 Great Russell Street
London WC1B 3DA

This paperback edition published in 2020

Typeset by Faber & Faber Limited
Printed and bound by CPI Group (UK) Ltd, Croydon, CR0 4YY

'Green Madrigal (I)', from Lynette Roberts: *Collected Poems*,
edited by Patrick McGuinness, Carcanet Press, 2005, is reproduced
by kind permission of Carcanet Press

A CIP record for this book
is available from the British Library

ISBN 978-0-571-34029-3

2 4 6 8 10 9 7 5 3 1

Peace, my stranger is a tree
Growing naturally through all its
Discomforts, trials and emergencies
Of growth.
It is green and resolved
It breathes with anguish
Yet it releases peace, peace of mind
Growth, movement.
It walks this greening sweetness
Throughout all the earth,
Where sky and sun tender its habits
As I would yours.

Lynette Roberts, 'Green Madrigal (I)'

1

Dead Papa Toothwort wakes from his standing nap an acre wide and scrapes off dream dregs of bitumen glistening thick with liquid globs of litter. He lies down to hear hymns of the earth (there are none, so he hums), then he shrinks, cuts himself a mouth with a rusted ring pull and sucks up a wet skin of acid-rich mulch and fruity detritivores. He splits and wobbles, divides and reassembles, coughs up a plastic pot and a petrified condom, briefly pauses as a smashed fibreglass bath, stumbles and rips off the mask, feels his face and finds it made of long-buried tannic acid bottles. Victorian rubbish.

Tetchy Papa Toothwort should never sleep in the afternoon; he doesn't know who he is.

He wants to kill things, so he sings. It sounds slow-nothing like tarmac bubbles popping in a heatwave. His grin takes a sticky hour. Cheering up, he chatters in the voice of a cultured fool to the dry papery wings and under-bark underlings, to the marks he left here last year, to the mice and larks, voles and deer, to the quaint memory of himself as cyclically reliable, as part of the country curriculum. He slips through one grim costume after another as he rustles and

trickles and cusses his way between trees. He walks a
few paces as an engineer in a Day-Glo vest. He takes
a step in a dinner suit, then an Anderson shelter, then
a tracksuit, then a rusted jeep bonnet, then a leather
skirt, but nothing works. He pauses as an exhaust
pipe, then squirms into the shape of a rabbit snare,
then a pissed-on nettle into pink-strangled lamb. He
plucks a blackbird from the sky and cracks open the
yellow beak. He peers into the ripped face as if it
were a clean pond. He flings the bird across the forest
stage, stands up woodlot bare, bushy, and stamps his
spalted feet. His body is a suit of bark-armour with
the initials of long-dead teenage lovers carved in the
surface. He clomps through the wood, wide awake and
hungry for his listening.

Only one thing can cheer up crotchety Toothwort
and that's his listening.

He slides across the land at precisely the speed of
dusk and arrives at his favourite spot. The village
sits up pretty to greet him, sponged in half-light.
He climbs into the kissing gate. He is invisible and
patient and about the size of a flea. He sits still.
He listens.
Here it is.

seedling

4

Human sound, tethered to his interest, dragged across the field, sucked into his great need.

Private property,   honeycomb

Gorgeous.

                    Shampoo in my eyes,   windfalls

A lovely time of day.

press pause, no sign of Dad, stinks in there, tilt your glass

Now it is around him, he reaches in and delicately pulls out threads, a conductor coaxing sound out of an orchestra,
                    planting stock
        bin it then

expertly, unhurried, like time slowly acting death upon an organism, little by little, listening. He hears his village turning itself over towards its bedtime,

                                        piss off Alan

much higher wattage, brilliant dreams,
                    fan-belt squeal

clean forgot milk

talking to old Peggy

every last mouthful,

weird time to be alive,

how are your knees, it's an astroturf-burn not cancer

Dad's livid, more gin than tonic,

autumn's a brutal surgeon,

**Dead Papa Toothwort exhales, relaxes,
lolls inside the stile, smiles and drinks it in, his
English symphony,**

rooks quacking, laminate the rota,

year 9s lost control,

Agnetta's piled on the pounds,

a sign up at Elm House,

my trusty friend Diarrhoea,

quick
kick-
about,

original windows, nip into town,

old people die,

satsuma p e e l down the street like a treasure trail,

littleshit,

interesting light,

Special Delivery and Signed For are not the same thing,

countries can grow wrong,

never seen a fella more coke-fucked,

choir clashes with Benders sadly,

horrid parents,

pretty in a smudgy kind of way,

last glass then bed,   blocked drains,

piggish ginger son who bullied our Aaron,

Iranian or something,

coming in   and out   like the wind,

Sheila's salted caramel rice pudding sweet Jesus I died and went to heaven

nine English pound,

he swims in it, he gobbles it up and wraps himself in it, he rubs it all over himself, he pushes it into his holes, he gargles, plays, punctuates and grazes, licks and slurps at the sound of it, wanting it fizzing on his tongue, this place of his,

apple like that, professor says so,   quiche au vomit,

the gate worn where she's leant on it seventy summers,

shrieking like sexed-up foxes,   he's a bum-bandit,

state of the toilets, fibre-optic, put our foot down,

foil on tray first,   fewer antibiotics healthier cows,

endless moaning,

sinister old wackjob, state of that scooter,   naff as shit tat,
Linda Liability,
nine blue constituencies in a chain of good sense,   you or me,
                    begging for a lift on Friday,
more ironing then a cuppa,
                    little word to the wise Ken, skutter,
Marxist knitters unite,   PlayStation's bust,
                    Dave has bucketloads of dahlias

Dead Papa Toothwort chews the noise of the place and waits for his favourite taste, but he hasn't got to it yet,

I was a schoolteacher so I know all about bumped heads,
          there are boyish saplings girly saplings and foot-high baby brackens,
     whatsup dapper two-chins,
               uprooting a load of bluebells for two days of prettiness,
Fat Pam on a scone and jam rampage,
                    told him buggered clutch, change channels,
useful compost,   text him back,
Roy's had another attack,   Yashvi collects on week-nights,
          affair enough look at his missus, over my dead body,
     I saw the carers going in but Jean said they were past that point,
sturdy jasmine,   twenty press-ups and a five-knuckle shuffle,
               hark at me planning a month ahead,
          jugs of run-off,
                              recycling bags, tombola,

8

bang out of order, pay-as-you-go, simply unwelcome, brings up
toxic masculinity every   single   book club,   El gaz pissed as a newt,

and then he hears it, clear and true, the lovely sound
of his favourite.
The boy.

> *It would have the head of a dolphin and the wings*
> *of a peregrine, and it would be a storm-warning*
> *beast, watching the weather while we sleep.*

Dead Papa Toothwort hugs himself with diseased
larch arms and dribbles cuckoo spit down his chin.
He grins. *The head of a dolphin and the wings of a peregrine!*
Surgical yearnings invade him, he wants to chop the
village open and pull the child out. Extract him.
Young and ancient all at once, a mirror and a key.
A storm-warning beast, watching the weather . . . He listens
to the boy for a while, his bedtime thoughts, his
goodnight words to his mother, his waking mind
trickling into visionary sleep. Then Dead Papa
Toothwort leaves his spot and wanders off, chuckling,
jangling in his various skins, wearing a tarpaulin
gloaming coat, drunk on the village, ripe with feeling,
tingling with thoughts of how one thing leads to
another again and again, time and again, with no such
thing as an ending.

LANNY'S MUM

In came the sound of a song,
warm on his creaturely breath.

My singing child,

bringing me gifts.

A second or two before I realise it's not him.

Lanny?

LANNY'S DAD

I sit at work in the city and the thought of him existing a sixty-minute train ride from me, going about his day in the village, carrying his strange brain around, seems completely impossible. It seems unlikely, when I'm at work, that we had a child and it is Lanny. If my parents were here they'd surely say, No Robert, you've dreamt him. Children aren't like that. Go back to sleep. Go back to work.

His school report said, 'Lanny has an innate gift for social cohesion. He will often calm a fraught classroom with a single well-timed joke or song.' I see, objectively, that this must be the case. It sounds like Lanny. But where did his gifts come from? Do I have the same gifts? What or who is supposed to manage and regulate Lanny and his gifts? Oh fuck, it's us. Who can have children and not go completely mad?

'Lanny is especially gifted with language and his World Book Day *Tarka the Otter* acrostic was shown to the headmaster and given an outstanding plus-stage gold elm sticker.'

What? What are any of you talking about? I want a sticker.

PETE

At that time I was into finding and cleaning the skeletons of dead things. Mostly birds. I would pull them apart, coat them in gold leaf, reassemble them wrongly and suspend them from wire frames. Little mobiles of badly made birds. I'd done a dozen or so. The gallery wanted something to show. To sell.

I was also taking casts of different barks. I was setting them in boxes with scraps of text.

Some drawings. Some half-decent prints. Sets. Quiet stuff.

She came down to the studio one morning and brought me a branch with two perfect arms. She'd seen a carved man I'd done.

We'd gone from chatting in the street now and then to her popping in for a tea once or twice a week. Sometimes with Lanny, sometimes alone. They'd only lived in the village a year or two.

She'd seen a rough-cut man I'd done, a Christ without a cross, and she'd seen the possibility of another in this fallen branch.

You are most kind, I said.
Pleasure, Pete, she said.

I liked her. Good for a natter. Warm, with a good eye for things. I often showed her my work and she had interesting things to say. She made me laugh, but she knew when to piss off. Seemed to know when I wasn't sociable.

She was an actor, had done plays, a bit of TV. She told stories about all that. About all those arseholes in that business. It never sounded a million miles from the art world back in the day.

She didn't miss the acting work but she got bored sometimes, when Lanny went to school, when her husband went in to the city. She was writing a book, she said. A murder thriller.

Sounds bloody horrid, I said.

It is very bloody and horrid, she said, but thrilling.

Often she would sit with me while I worked. She'd bought one of my pieces, without me knowing, from the gallery. One of my good big reliefs. I said I would have given her mate's rates if I'd known and she said, Exactly, Pete.

I liked her.

She used to fiddle with whatever was lying around.

Bits of wire. A pencil. Some twigs.

Make something, by all means, I once said.

Oh no I'm hopeless with visual things, she said.

And I remember thinking what a strange and sad thing that was to say.

Hopeless, with visual things.

Someone must have said something to her to make a notion like that stick.

I thought of my mum. Someone said to my mother once when she was very young that she couldn't hold a tune. So she never sang or whistled in her life. I can't sing, she'd say.

Wasn't til a lot later after she was gone that I recognised that for the preposterous notion it was. *Can't sing.*

So she's sat at my table poking crumbled lichen into a pile while we chat about the new glass cube monstrosity being built on Sheepridge Hill.

I'm watching her.

First she makes a neat shape. Flattens it. Divides in two. Pinches it into two lines. Nudges the two lines in and out of contact so she's got a little row of green-grey teeth. Pats it down rectangular and uses her nail to make the edges clean, then she dabs a perfect circle in the middle with a wet fingertip.

Hopeless with visual things, but sitting there keeping a small pile of dried moss moving into half a dozen lovely shapes, absently making pictures on my kitchen table.

She looks up at me and says she knows I'm busy and she knows I'm famous, but if it isn't too stupid an idea could I give young Lanny some art lessons.

Art lessons: bollocks, I thought.

I told her that much as I liked the lad and enjoyed my chats with him, I couldn't imagine anything worse than teaching art.

I'm a miserable solitary bastard and can hardly hold a pencil, I said.

And she laughed, and said she understood, and then off she drifted in that nice way she has. Responsive to the light, I would call it. The type of person who is that little bit more akin to the weather than most people, more obviously made of the same atoms as the earth than most people these days seem to be. Which explains Lanny.

So she left, that morning, and I sat and breathed in the atmosphere of her visit and thought a lot about women

growing up, being a girl in the world, and I missed my
mum then, and my sister, and some women I've known,
and I carefully laid tiny flakes of gold onto the skull of a
robin and hummed 'Old Sprig of Thyme' to myself.

LANNY'S MUM

In came the sound of a song,
warm on his creaturely breath,
and he snuggled against me, climbing up on my lap,
wrapping himself around my neck.

I said, Lanny enters stage left, singing, stinking of pine
tree and other nice things.

I thought, Please don't get too grown-up for these
hugs, my little geothermal bubba.

LANNY'S DAD

If I get the 7.21 I miss breakfast with Lanny, but
I avoid Carl Taylor and usually get a seat. If I get
the 7.41 I'll see Lanny but Carl Taylor will find me
on the platform and I'll have to hear about Susan
Taylor and the clever Taylor girls and which subjects
they're doing for GCSE and we'll probably have to
stand, someone's armpit, someone's fold-up bike, Carl
Taylor's trundling newsfeed mixing with someone's
tinny headphone music.

Down the village street, hit the bowl of the crossroads good and fast for a belly wobble, up Ghost Pilot Lane, through Ashcote, dual carriageway all the way into town. Assuming there are no tractors or cyclists I can be at the station in under twenty minutes. My personal best is fourteen. If I slow down on Ghost Pilot Lane there might be deer on the road and I can stop for a minute and watch them. Or I can honk to warn them I'm coming and hit 70 or 80, windows down to blast myself awake and enjoy the car. I may as well enjoy the car, it cost me enough and it spends most of its life parked, waiting for me.

Sometimes, if I've driven fast, I have five minutes in the station car park and I sit and talk to my vehicle. Thank you, I'll say. Pleasure doing business with you Sir. Nice one, mate. Bucephalus, you absolute beauty you're the best horse ever. This is what commuting is. Small pleasures coaxed from playing the routine like a game. Little tricks of the part-time countryman. It might be soul-destroying. I might be a bit pitiful. I don't know.

I have a drawing by Lanny stuck above my desk. It's me in a cape, flying above a skyline and it says, 'Where does Dad go every day? Nobody knows.'

LANNY'S MUM

Pete knocked on the door.

Got past old Peggy with no interrogation.

Congratulations, Pete, but she'll get you on the way back. She's worried about people feeding the kites. Cup of tea?

He looked down at his boots and tugged his beard.

I won't. But look. I was thinking after you left the other night. I was thinking I'm a miserable old bastard, and what on earth's to stop me being less of one. I wouldn't know how to teach and I hated being taught myself. But if what you're asking is whether Lanny can come and sit in my kitchen, use my paper, draw with me, chat about what I do, then why not. He's a lovely fella and I could do with the company. It might even do me some good. So how about it, after school Mondays or Wednesdays?

Oh you're wonderful Pete. And you'd let us pay you?

Absolutely not. No fucken way, dear. Get your rich husband to buy one of my fiddly gold birds when they go up next year.

Well, you're very kind. Lanny will be so pleased. Wednesday, please.

Pete crunched off down the driveway. He raised a backward hand and shouted:

Wednesday four o'clock. I shall be waiting!

DEAD PAPA TOOTHWORT

Dead Papa Toothwort lies underneath a nineteenth-
century vicar's wife and fiddles with the roots of a yew
in her pelvis. He loves the graveyard. He listens . . .

when I die make me into fatballs for the birds,   fine so long as Jimmy's mum says so,

ten new highlighters from petty cash,

Dylan needs a dimmer switch on his temper,

a dick that big should be on a leash,

open-plan kitchen,   floral prints,

Tom hasn't been at all well,   a whippet's good nature,

over-extended, new tractors new fences,

all pumped up and shiny like a greased pig,   ten of the rubber spatulas

from the door-to-door crim,   heavy limey soil,

she can't pour Guinness but we forgive that

more to life than the interweb,   on account of her titties,

what will kill Brian Gould is old-fashioned self-pity

**Dead Papa Toothwort remembers
when they built this church,**

compline and meditation, he's a fool to do it on the bank holiday,

haven't seen it yet Jan but I am grateful for the prior warning,

rotting mouse, biotech my arse I kill pigs for a living,

wife-swap pampas grass, hence the moniker
Mad Jean,

Dr Horvath has seen to my haemorrhoids,
I'm apocalyptic about the bees,
    salt of the earth,
                oi va voi here comes creepy Da Vinci

lice again,   Trinidadian but everyone
                                                assumes Jamaican,
shiny new car, scruple-free human, nowhere to park,
                    hedges will be that man's Achilles heel,
        fresh out of Silk Cut,

            stone from afar, flint from round here, timber
from these very woods, local boys, bring down the
bodgers and set them to pews, set them to floral
ornaments, a hymn board with ivy corners, an altar
table with — yes indeed, there he is, a Green Man's
head, grinning at the baptised and married, the bored
and the dead, biting down on limewood belladonna,

vomit behind the hall,
    parochial representatives of the laity or gossips as I call them,
    pseudo-legend Margaret,   talking to Peggy
                        on the market seven months,   for hours,
half a dozen dogshit bins,   everyone knows everyone,
                    a whole country with short-man complex,
the news is not good on Tom's scare,   Gyppo alert, we raised £45.67,
    it's not Julie it's Jolie would you believe,
                    the smell of that Philadelphus god almighty,

cheers for that Ma, stout gives me the runs,

snogging like starving goblins,
no more cynicism thank you gentlemen, my arm smelt of moss,
someone is regularly crying themselves to sleep in Thackeray House,
was woodland once
will be woodland again,

discount fertiliser   *pretentious prick,*
you'll have a stampede,
beautifully presented Victorian house with views of the idyllic
Stowely wildflower meadow,

mind of a child

He has been represented on keystones,
decorative stencils, tattoos, the cricket club logo, he
has been every English trinket and trash, moral for
cash, mascot and curse. He has been in story form
in every bedroom of every house of this place. He is
in them like water. Animal, vegetable, mineral. They
build new homes, cutting into his belt, and he pops
up adapted, to scare and define. In this place he is as
old as time.

PETE

We commence our lessons.

We are indoors because mile-wide slabs of rain romp across the valley.

Palette-knife smears of bad weather rush past the window.

Two chairs pulled up to the kitchen table.

Snug. Fire on. Radio 3.

Two pads, two pencils, a tumbler of juice, a mug of tea.

Ah, Lanny, my friend, look at these blank pages.
Don't you feel like God at the start of the ages?
You could do anything.

So GO! I said. Draw me a man.

What man?

Any. Just a person. Something human. I tossed a little coin in my head between tree and man and it landed man, so let's start with that.

His shoulders roll over, right slightly higher as his arms hug the page and he starts to scratch away, with a soft hum-come-whisper of half words and trickling bits of melody. Concentrating. He's not a rusher.

He scratches his head, sits up and slides the drawing over. Furrowed brow.

Right, let's look. Yup, I'd say that was a man all right. Nicely done. Now let's talk our way around him a bit and see what's what.

The grimace of concentration is gone and Lanny's face is wide open, curious and listening. His eyes are like spring hornbeam, a very fresh green.

Right, Lanny. Where do your arms come out? You've got this bloke's arms coming out the side of his body, what do you reckon?

We turn sideways and spread our arms, two aeroplanes at the kitchen table. Lanny smiles and nods down to his shoulder and then starts a new pair of arms emerging from the right height, not out the poor bastard's centre.

Now the head, Lanny. Might I ask you to consider your own self and see if there's anything between your head and your chest?

He grins and points to his neck, feigning discovery.

We laugh. We're pleased. We chink drinks and raise a toast to the better-looking image of a man.

Long after he's gone, after that first lesson, I sit and think.

I try and recreate the noises Lanny makes, his part-song chant:

'Limmon aah, bitter car, lemmen arr, fennem arr, mennem are, witter kah, fitterkarr, but chakka but chakka but chakka, limmon aah . . .'

I suppose it's some TV theme tune or pop song I don't know. Maybe it's just Lanny taking things from wherever he's been listening, soaking up the sounds of this world and spinning out threads of another.

I wait.

Breeze-obedient balls of dust and fluff huddle in the corners of the kitchen.

I remember how grey I felt in the busy days, when the work was selling suddenly. When people wanted things from me all the time. Knew my name. London. And I feel my way back before that, to days of clarity like this. To being a boy.

I remember an elderly lady once showed me my own drawing of a man and asked me to consider where, anatomically, my arms began.

That lady is a long time dead.

English seasons roll out of bed.

LANNY'S MUM

Lanny dances into the room, singing, smelling of the outdoors.

Dooo yoooou know, he says, that clownfish are all born male and when the queen dies one of the men turns into a female and becomes the new queen? So what came first, male or queen?

I'd say queen, funny bean.

I wrap him up in a hug.

What are you up to, Mum?

I don't answer, and he wanders off, tracing some current of curiosity, following his little hunches or queries back out into the garden.

I couldn't tell him. I couldn't say, Lanny I'm writing a scene about a man who corners a woman at a party. He whispers into her ear that she is a *little bitch*. He presses his knee against her crotch.

I am making terrible things up to entertain people. A publisher has paid me a good sum of money to write a novel about abuse and revenge, based on a twelve-page sample I wrote in which a woman poisons a powerful man and throws his body in a furnace.

What a perplexing thing this suddenly seems to be, in the holidays, when my little boy is home from school, when I could be in the garden with him listening to his clownfish facts.

I watch him hanging upside down in the plum tree.

My husband queries the morality of crime fiction. He says I am glamorising things. Glamorising what, he doesn't yet know, because he hasn't read the book. I'm only playing devil's advocate, he says then, as if his interventions have been hugely inspiring or constructive. Devil's advocate, losing his signal going through a tunnel, asking what's for his tea. Devil's advocate, snoring next to me while I sit up reading.

I'm a bad enough mother. I'm a good enough crime fiction writer. Lanny is nothing to do with the sickness of the human spirit I write about. He might see contamination coming and step gracefully aside. He will not become a malevolent or unhappy person because of what was in his mother's Word documents. This is all in my head. Lanny is all in his own head. Who is judging me? I daren't consider it.

Does my husband sit on the train and worry that the crushing dullness of Collateralised Loan Obligations might be leaking into Lanny? I doubt it. Does he feel disgusted and ashamed that his phone, which Lanny

uses to look up videos of blue whales, is the same
phone on which he watches porn, sadly whacking
away at himself in the bathroom while I pretend to
be dreaming of murder plots? No, he doesn't. Such
burdens are always hers.

LANNY'S DAD

How's little Lenny? asks Charles, my line manager.

Lanny.

How is he, still mad as a March hare?

I have an urge to punch this man, my twat-of-a-boss,
for speaking of my son like this. But where did he get
the idea that Lanny was mad? From me. And why does
he think he can speak to me this way about my family?
Because of me.

I gaze down at London from the twenty-third floor
of this heated glass box. It's as if a gigantic child has
vandalised a city-sized circuit board, chucked some
bricks in, sprayed it with dirt, started painting it but
given up. Trains chuffing in and out, little people
hurrying for cover or lunch or greenery. It takes itself
so seriously. It's ludicrous. I love it.

The village we live in is so small. Fewer than fifty
redbrick cottages, a pub, a church, the little council

cottages like a breakaway settlement, a few bigger houses dotted about. The space between buildings, the space around the buildings, that space is a preposterous thought, considered from here. How can that possibly work, that little cluster of homes surrounded by trees and fields?

My annoyance fades. Lanny would be thrilled to be compared to a March hare, leaping in the long grass, boxing his own reflection. A bringer of strange dreams, skipping about the wide open village.

He's great thanks, Charles. And yes, bonkers. Totally bonkers. Gets it from his mother.

PETE

We do some lessons outdoors while the weather's good.

What's your favourite season, Lanny?

Autumn.

Ah good, mine too.

We trudge away from the village, through the gap in the hedge where Sampson's miles of stubbly set-aside meet the back end of the school playing field, and the land bends away.

We stop by the Elvis Hair Hawthorn.

This, Lanny, is a significant place.

Why?

This is the first point at which you can no longer be seen. The village is always watching, but past this point you're beyond their gaze.

Either side of us, woods. Ahead of us, hills. Counties lapping falsely at each other over the stone plates which rough-and-tumbled to form this gentle landscape. Some very old trees round this way. Saints.

We tramp down the steep-walled chalk and moss run, tree roots like sea monsters lining our route, and we discuss the passing of time.

I tell Lanny about the ghost of Ben Hart who runs up and down this track trying to find his beloved. Headless Ben Hart calling out for his girl. I'm only teasing, trying to shit him up a bit, but he replies in all sincerity, Brilliant, I hope we meet him.

We stop and draw the tangled lines of beech foundations, under us stone and bone, above us the burnt sienna canopy, starting to crisp.

This was the way to a hillfort, once.

The boy does well with charcoal. Likes the way it smudges.

Making shadows, he says.

We go back and experiment, printing with skeletal leaves, where insects and time have stripped away we build with ink, we drip and dip and make a decent new mess.

Often as he works Lanny says strange and wonderful things, mumblings, puzzling things for a child to say –

I'm a million cameras, even when I'm sleeping, clicking, clicking, every second something is growing and changing. We are little arrogant flashes in a grand magnificent scheme.

I burst out laughing.

You what? Where did you get that from?

Not sure, he says.

He tilts his head and some half-formed secret thing skips out of his mouth and disappears into the space between us.

Times like this Lanny seems almost possessed.

DEAD PAPA TOOTHWORT

He has some rules, like never trust cats, never kiss
a badger, always lick a new flavour pesticide, only
eat what yields to a twist, and always make sure
at the summer fête to get amongst the folk who
dress up as Toothwort. Every year in the costumes,
in the posture, in the ligaments and juices of his
worshippers, he himself must move

hideous racket, thought they could sell the old barn,

odd couple,   Rodney is a liar darling,

the bastard came down in the storm, egg on your face,

Shrita suggested   his dog's called Sir Walter Raleigh,

second week in August, sort of a silty residue, posh twat,

I went into town, Skivey Nick's been fired,   creepy little single child,

deregulation is never the rural way, skylark population dwindling,

it's us versus them and it's always been thus,

what next Polish adverts in the parish mag,

gazing up at the sky like she can't bear the sight of us,

Mark smelt of rivers,   we don't welcome hobbyists Malcolm,

thirsty work listening to
all this, more talk than ever, he is so thirsty from
watching all the adorable decomposition and keeping
up with all the grinding lyric-practical nonsense of
their days,

a sort of   backpacked round Asia and came back as much *of a twat as he left,*

belch-like yelp,   throw a muntjac onto the bonfire,

solar panels my arse,   Uncle Phil the freemason-slash-fascist,

a lemonade top not a bloody shandy,   fancy netting,

we can't do Stoppard two years running,

trust him with your kid,   no insurance no exchange amigo,

man so sick of Trappy beats,

see if we get any rain, a crevice not a pothole,

I said as much at the Easter meeting, *chompy Ron,*

let us resurrect happy hardcore meine Schwester,

Big no-biscuits scandal at the stay and play,

dreams of meeting a celebrity, pills and powders Saturday,

making little lamps for Diwali, Ivy is the enemy of old walls,

Guinness for Paul *Cider for Barnsey*   and a Stella for me,

He peers into the kitchen of the boy's house
and watches the child drinking milk and he sees
the cold liquid pouring into the boy's belly, trickle
puddle pond lake, into the cellular cathedrals of
his organs, into his bones. Dead Papa Toothwort is
drunk on the hydration and nourishment of the boy.
Glorious, he sings, as he swings his way back into the
woods, flinging himself in thirty-foot arcs between
telegraph poles, dressed as a barn owl with car-tyre
arms, *Glorious trick of the species.*

LANNY'S MUM

Robert said I should try again to offer Pete some money.

We argued about it.

He brought it up at a dinner party with Greg and Sally.

Tell me, he said, is it or is it not weird that Mad Pete is giving free art lessons to Lanny?

Don't call him that, I said, because I think it's horrid, and I dislike the cruelty Robert performs when he's drinking, when he is showing off to friends.

I vote totally weird, said Sally.

I vote not in the slightest bit weird, said Greg. He's Peter Blythe, he was pretty famous back in the day, so you're getting a bargain. And if they get on well, and he needs the company, go for it.

'Needs the company' is exactly why it's not right. It's unprofessional, said Sally.

Exactly, says Robert, waving his expensive salad tongs. *Who* needs the company? Are we lending out our son to stave off Pete's loneliness? Like conversational meals on wheels for sad old artists?

Oh fuck off, Robert, I said. Is it beyond your shrunken world view to imagine that something *nice* might exist without money ever needing to change hands?

Glances.

Awkward silence.

Go on Robert, I think to myself, deal with your angry wife and your weird son.

Bloody hell, love. Fine. I just think you should insist on making it a formal thing, that's all. In my *shrunken world view*, I think that's the right thing to do.

Sally, who is a fool, giggled and said, Raw nerve Rob, and Robert and I shared a flickering and bitter conspiratorial glance because he detests being called Rob.

So I knocked on Pete's door.

Come in, he said.

I won't, I'm killing someone important in my book. I just popped down to give you this.

And what's this?

Some money for Lanny's art lessons.

Oh no, you mustn't.

We feel we ought to, I said. And I was proud of myself for saying 'we', proud of my insincere solidarity with Robert.

I feel you absolutely ought not to, said Pete. As I said before, just buy a golden bird in the spring. I won't accept payment for something I'm enjoying so much. Your son has brought me joy. He's got a good eye. I like showing him things.

He loves it, I said. He sits in his room and draws, and sings.

Good, said Pete. I should be paying you!

I walked up the village street, pretending to be on my phone so as not to have to stop and chat to Peggy about the coming moral apocalypse, and I squirmed in the imaginary space between how Robert would react to a comment like that – *I should be paying you!* – and how I wanted to hear it. I wanted to be charmed by a comment like that. I wanted dinner parties with Pete, not Greg and Sally. Dinners where nobody speaks for a while, where we talk about books we've read, and someone falls asleep and it's not weird or eccentric, it's just slow and kind, unhurried and accepting. Acceptance is a fascination of mine. I ask at every parent's evening, Is Lanny accepted? Well-liked? Settling in?

And his teacher says, Lanny? You make him sound like an illegal alien. Lanny's wonderful, absolutely at ease and well-liked, as if he's been here forever.

PETE

I hate the smell of metal, Pete.

He mumbles as we sit, dangling legs over a chalky ledge, up in Hatchett Wood. The village is a cruciform grid with the twin hearts of church and pub in the middle. Four hundred people sheltered from the fields, clinging to each other for warmth. Redbrick boxes and the outlying farms, the big house, the timber yard, a handful of scruffy agricultural blemishes on the green patchwork skin of this area. If you looked at the village from above and it was a man, then his hair would be Hatchett Wood. We'd be sitting on top of his brain.

The smell of metal scares me, he says.

At once I am a child again, smelling my palms.

Blood iron, coins, nails and pins.

War men with bullets and rusty hinge grins.

The smell of metal lingers on my lips and on my fingers.

My father would have me count his coppers on a Sunday. Memory swings like a hard dirt rudder then slips up with a boom and a crack and catches the wind.

God, Lanny, I say. I hate the smell of metal too. I despise the smell of metal on my hands.

Why do they call you Mad Pete?

Hah! I dunno mate. I don't think my covering all the trees up by the cricket pitch with plaster-of-Paris after the Great Storm did me any favours. Anyway, I don't mind it. Mad Pete. Better than Bad Pete.

Or Sad Pete.

Well yes. Isn't fair though, given how fuckin' – excuse my language – given how insane some of the folk in this village are.

Like Jean Coombe.

Exactly! She wears a Santa costume every day of the year and carries a golf club in her wicker basket and I don't hear anyone calling her Mad Jean.

LANNY'S DAD

I'm awake, thinking of quarterly dividends and Olympic women cyclists. I hear the crunch of gravel, too heavy for a fox, too light for a man. I hop out of bed, pad across the room and peek out of the curtain.

What the hell?

I tiptoe hurriedly across the bedroom, out onto the landing, down the stairs, avoiding the creaky step. I'm not sure why I'm being secretive. I go through the kitchen and out of the open back door.

He's at the bottom of the driveway turning onto the lawn.

I follow at a safe distance.

He walks to the old oak.

He kneels and presses his ear to it. This whole thing is lit by the security light, and beautiful, like a film set.

Lanny lies down, talking to the base of the tree.

I wander over, heavy footfall and a cough so as not to surprise.

Lanny? Lanny you're sleepwalking.

He turns to me, green eyes flashing, wide awake.

Oh wow, do I sleepwalk?

What? Well, I don't know. What the hell are you doing out here?

I'm awake, Dad!

Yes, I realise that now, Lan. I'm wondering what you're doing out here. I assumed you were sleepwalking. It's the middle of the night.

I heard the girl in the tree.

What?

There's a girl living under this tree. She's lived here for hundreds of years. Her parents were cruel to her so she hid under this tree and she's never come out.

OK, nutbar. Come on.

He offers no resistance as I scoop him up. He's freezing cold.

As we crunch back up the drive I tell him, Lanny, you shouldn't wander about in the dark.

Have you ever heard her?

No. I think you've imagined it. There's nobody living in the tree.

I carry him up and lie him down, cover him with his duvet, add another blanket, give him his stuffed polar bear.

Dad?

Go to sleep now.

Dad?

What, Lanny?

Which do you think is more patient, an idea or a hope?

I'm suddenly really annoyed. He's too old for shit like this. Or too young. It's fucking silly.

Go to sleep Lanny, and don't get out of bed. We'll talk about this in the morning.

I lie awake worrying, picturing my son lying on the cold grass whispering to a tree. Which do you think is more patient, an idea or a hope? What's wrong with him?

PETE

It's Lanny's idea, a game he plays with his folks in the car. We are to tell a story, one line at a time.

We are drawing a bowl of plums and I'm trying to get him to slow down. I'm asking him not to panic if what he gets on the page doesn't seem to relate to what he sees. Start again. Ease up. Loosen your wrist. I tell him the best representation of a plum ever created might not bear any resemblance to any plum the artist ever saw. Just look at them and think about their plum-ness, the essence of the plum as a physical plum in your space, light bouncing off the plum and into your eyes, and try a few things out and see what feels plummy, gently nudge a plum into being, don't demand it.

He raises one eyebrow at me then looks at the plums. I almost pity the poor plums sitting there in the bowl with no defences against our joint scrutiny.

I start the game:

Once upon a time there was a man called Abel Stain.

And Lanny replies without missing a beat, The Fable of Abel Stain.

Is that your line or are you just chipping in with it?

Sorry, he says. That's what we can call it. It's a good title.

Right you are.

Me: This is The Fable of Abel Stain. Once upon a time there was a man called Abel Stain.

Lanny: He had three daughters and they were all really pretty.

Me: But horrible. Two of them were horrible, one of them was nice.

Lanny: The nice one was called Barbara.

I cackle.

Sorry, sorry, Lanny. Took me by surprise that's all. I did not expect her to be called Barbara. Hang on I'm getting a beer.

I go to the larder and open a bottle of stout. I come back and Lanny has got his hair all swept over his face and he's puffing on his pencil like it's a Gauloise in a holder and he says,

Halloo, my name's Barbara and I am much nicer than my 'orrible sisters.

I guffawspit beer all over the nice outlines of plums I've drawn.

DEAD PAPA TOOTHWORT

He is in and out of shadow, moss-socks, pebble-dash
skin, peering in the village hall looking at pictures
of himself in the yearly competition. No more Jack
in the green ale-tap Toothworts with bushy faces,
these are comedy DPTs, nasty charmless things with
guns, with fangs, with knives for hands, there is one
with dead rabbits tied around his waist (those were
the days). But they are based on fear imported, these
beasts, on TV terrors, games and comics, untouched
by genuine belief. He fondly remembers how much
more frightening he was when the village children
drew him green and leafy, born of dark gaps in
Sunday school nightmares, choked by tendrils growing
out of his mouth, threat and agony growing together,
tree demon, uncle and dad, king of the hawthorn and
hops, harvest and hope, threat of starvation,

Say Your Prayers and Be Good Too, Or Dead Papa Toothwort Is Coming for You.

      One of the pictures represents him simply as
a smiling old man with a beard. It's shocking. Dead
Papa Toothwort grins and whispers, *That's my boy,*
vandalism pure and simple,

   foreign woodpeckers, cheaper cassocks,

      she was in a film with whatsisname from you know and *he works in fin*

Willis sisters didn't get the myxomatosis memo, never actually did

    another tidy premium bond *win,*   *an undercoat,*

mowing upholstery fencing you name it,

        Paul's not-entirely-riveting lecture on the old colliery,

cock-off grandad, band practice you smelly tosspots, lesser-spotted council van,

someone is regularly screaming at their wife in Cobb Close,

       unaccompanied minors,

Glenda and I are withdrawing our support for the bell rope renovation project,

agricultural consultancy my arse,

   bunning with Oscar you should come along,

before the bypass you could watch the frogs make their merry way,

worst plant sale in a decade,

**In another picture he has
dripping stumps for hands and words curl around
him, like the quilted prayer banners they don't make
any more, for the hopeless stories of Jesus they don't
tell any more,**

Chop chop, knock knock, Toothwort comes with his chopping block,

   chop chop, knock knock, he'll boil your bones for his broth and stock

      yes he earns a big salary but the school is Ofsted outstanding,

toodle-pip my soaps are starting,

lord snooty comb-over and his blonde bimbo,

   descended from bird-starvers, barbed wire is the only answer,

  hushing his Saab, berea Locală e naşpa you know like shit taste,

the kid's a f r e a k,   holy communion-Eucharist-even s o n g,

bass-line bass-line it's never not jump-up time,

46

endless click smack whack of the Bowen kid trying to kick-flip,
gutters blocked by rotting squirrel,
    I recommend sturdy Veronica for a splash of colour in your borders,
        impromptu meeting of the watercolour society,
mad old coot, *I don't mind them if they pay their taxes,*

  jaunty little bit of topiary,

He leaves the village riding the smells from the
kitchens, spinning and surfing, wafting and curling,
from Jenny's lasagne to Larton's microwave stroganoff,
Derek's hotpot-for-one, such rich sauces, so much
sugar, was never so varied as this, not-very-recently-
dead meat dressed in fancy flavours, he laughs, funny
busy worker bees of the village stuffing their faces
and endlessly rebuilding and replacing things. All
they are is bags of shopping and bags of rubbish. He
takes such offence to the smell of Pam Foy's stir-in
jalfrezi sauce that he tears a bit of his nightmare skin
off and shoves it through her window. A truly horrid
dream. Sleep well Pam, he chuckles, as he floats
homeward across the field.

LANNY'S MUM

I pick Lan up from school and we go home and I settle in to my work and a little while later I hear a thump from his room so I go up and I say, Oh I thought you'd gone to Pete's, are you not going today?

He is sitting on his bed. He looks up at me and his face crumples in on itself like a piece of heated paper and he starts crying.

Lanny? I kneel in front of him with my hands on his little golden downy-haired knees, his bruised and grass-stained boy's knees.

Lanny, what's wrong?

He scrubs and dabs at his eyes, rolling his fists in his tears.

Nothing.

Lanny, what's wrong? Tell me.

I . . . nothing.

Poppet. What's happened? You can tell me anything.

He breathes and shudders and wipes his blotched and snotty face.

I broke something of Pete's.

Lanny is so embarrassed he curls in on himself. His bean-plant grace has been replaced by gangling discomfort and the thought flits past me that he is simply growing up, shedding his fairy skin. I can't visualise Lanny as a teenager.

I can't imagine this boy becoming a man.

What did you break?

His Victorian stereo-thing.

A stereo?

No, the magic 3D photo machine, with the eye box, the eye box bit fell off and the glass is broken and I just put it back and I didn't say anything.

Do you mean a stereoscope?

With the two pictures becoming 3D.

Lanny, sweetheart. Firstly, it was an accident, and secondly Pete is very fond of you and I'm sure he'd rather you just told him. It's always best to be honest.

Exactly! I didn't tell him, I just sneaked off. Like a liar. It's so rude.

Enough of this. It is not *so* rude. Come. Now, come with me.

We go downstairs, put our shoes on, and leave. We stride down the road. We don't talk, but Lanny sticks to my side in a way he hasn't for years. He is obedient and nervous, not the free-range verge-clambering son I am accustomed to.

We knock.

Pete opens the door and he has bright white arms. Plaster arms.

Maestro! I thought you'd stood me up. Maestro's Mother! To what do I owe the pleasure?

We go in and Pete washes his arms and shows us the chalk-white skull he has been modelling on bones of wire. He makes tea and we sit at his table.

Pete, Lanny would like to admit something to you.

Oh gawd this sounds ominous. Been stealing my valuable artworks have you?

There is a moment like a cello note, then. Warm and wooden and full of other things. Nobody speaks but we are all listening.

Lanny fidgets. Pete looks at me and his blue eyes are all trust and twinkle. He reminds me of an old Cornish fishing boat.

He smiles. Come on then, lad, the suspense is killing me.

I broke your stereoscope.
My what?

I fiddled with the eye bit to make it closer together
and the whole top bit fell off and the glass inside is
smashed.

LANNY. The stereoscope?

Pete's eyes pop in mock-outrage and he clenches his
fists.

Good god, Lanny, that stereoscope, *my* precious
stereoscope, was handed down to me by my Great-
great-great-Aunt Oxfam Charity Shop and cost me
all of about £4.50. I could not give two shits that you
broke it. Jesus Christ, I thought something bad had
happened!

Lanny is as pink as a radish and looks from Pete to me
and starts to giggle.

Um, phew?

Phew! says Pete, and roars with laughter, banging the
table and reaching over to cuff Lanny on the head.

Pheweeeee, I say. There, poppet, what did I tell you? No
need for a total mental breakdown.

Crisis over, says Pete. Now roll up those little sleeves of
yours and let's make some mess.

DEAD PAPA TOOTHWORT

Dead Papa Toothwort, local historian, seventy-fourth-generation cultural humus sifter, is giving a bright orange Fanta bottle top a tour of the village.

Keep up, chap, still lots to see.

He does the voices

(this place had a distinctive accent until quite recently, "yop buck", you can still hear it on a handful of village tongues).

He tells the fascinated plastic cap of times past. He resuscitates tales and teases stories from the molecular memory of the village.

Chopped into the briar here, was all hazel, some holly, Danish axes, Pip lost a finger, underfoot here was the old village road, before our Black Death party, this hump is the back wall of a dwelling even I can't remember and here a notable font of not-local stone, this was all open field, Matilda rode Wilelmus here and snapped his little weapon, hedged into half-acres, small furlongs for ugly ploughs, hawthorn went in, half and half again, was a pond here, was a Roman soldier raped by his primus pilus here, was the fact of us being seven miles from the mill that defined

us, was beech to the left of me – beech to the right
– beech coffin bury me – beech for my wife, ah yes
those were the days, yes those pretty little black bags
decorating the hedge are in fact dogshit bags courtesy
of Brian and Fay and their beagles, paid our licence,
paid our tax . . .
Such a beautiful place, **interrupts the Fanta cap . . .**
BEAUTIFUL? **screams Toothwort, pausing the tour,**
taking the form of a notable English poet with a
waterproof map and a breathable turquoise jacket:
Beauty is what, my semi-synthetic friend? Illness, decay
and exploitation? A tapestry of small abuses, fights and
littering, lake-loads of unready chemicals piped into my
water bed, greed and decline, preaching teaching crying
dying and walking the fucking dogs, breeding and
needing and working and . . .
The Fanta lid is quietly whistling a roundhead ballad.
He has stopped listening to Toothwort the bore,
Toothwort the over-the-top audio guide.
Roger de St John once rode this way to look at some
hedging and was heard to say 'nice run to the valley',
good scope for poaching, haunted rowan moves a yard
a year, Saxon boundary, concrete silage bunker, too
many children for only one teacher, each year more
demand for privacy, high-speed broadband, cures
for limp dicks and depression, insecure boundaries,
imported vegetables, nostalgia for expansion,

Dead Papa Toothwort sways in the breeze and the many-centuries-long furrows of his remembrance all tilt him towards the child; Strong Henry Beresford born 1426 cut down three thousand oaks in his lifetime, and the boy understands that effort and that labour. Shifty Giles Morgan born 1956, purveyor of abundant natural light for kitchens and low-impact loft conversions, he will die in his bed from rotten lungs, and the boy sees that in sequence and fairness. Runny Jenny Savage born 1694 wasn't a witch, was no such thing, was simply a curious cook, and the boy feels that too, comprehends without knowing whether they are centuries dead or alive next door. The boy understands. He builds his magical camp in the woods as a gift to them all. They should worship him! He is in tune with the permanent, can feel a community's tensile frame. Do you see? His intuition?

Lanny Greentree, your miracle ribs remind me of me. Like me. Do you see?

The Fanta top has gone.

Toothwort is alone. He's tiny, the pulse of a robin redbreast, not even that, the empty air where a robin was earlier in the day, the atom-memory of the pulse, smaller than light.

The boy knows me.
He really truly knows me.

PETE

We're in the woods. Given the choice, Lanny will always choose the woods.

I've told him about the weird Willis sisters, growing devil rabbits in their greenhouses to spy on us.

He's come right back at me with a story about forests knowing if a person's good or bad. A decent human they'll keep alive, guiding them to water and food. A bad person they'll kill in a day, all forces of the forest united against the impure imposter.

Could say the same of a big city, I say.

I'm scratching away in my book, nice new fine-liner pen, hatching, bits and bobs, enjoying being wrapped up in my coat, drawing the beech trees' gnarled little belly-buttons, could be old hills from above, could be warts, trying to get Lanny to enjoy using a pen, not being able to rub out, he's a fanatic for rubbing out, trying to show him how you can keep on building, use the dark, wrestle a thing back if you've taken a wrong turn, I want him to enjoy making marks, I want him to let his wrist go a little bit. Hang on, where is he?

Lanny?

I am alone.

His sketchbook sits open next to me. There's a nervous charge in the air. Something guilty. Like when you meet a deer in the wood and the deer disappears and you're left standing there all clumping human noise, and there's shame in that.

Oh god I've lost him.

Where is he?

Lanny?

Then from way up above me,

There are bees up here!

There are bees up here!

Pete, there are bees up here!

He is fifty foot high, clambering about the crown of a vast chestnut, foreshortened like a painted trompe l'oeil angel in the rigging of the wood.

Above him I can see a sparrowhawk pinned to the ultramarine.

Stay there and hold on tight, you little nutter, I wanna draw you!

LANNY'S MUM

In comes Lanny clicking and murmuring like the peculiar transmitter-device he is. I minimise the document so he can't read over my shoulder; a scene in which my protagonist has pushed a corrupt politician in front of a train and then – hours later – found a little piece of his cranium stuck to her V&A Museum tote bag.

Hello poppet, I thought you were playing football with Archie and Toby?

Nope. Got bored. Can I tell you a secret?

I'd love that, yes please.

I almost told Pete but I want it to be a surprise, and I don't want to tell Dad because he might be cross.

Right, and what makes you so sure I won't be?

You're never very cross.

I could start now. Go on, what is it?

I'm building a bower.

A what?

Like bowerbirds do. I'm building a camp full of all the best stuff I've found, like a tiny museum of magic things.

Ah, yes, I know what you mean. In the garden? Have you started?

Nope, somewhere secret. I've been working on it for ages.

Is Archie helping?

Nope. No way.

And the bowerbird makes this for his lady, right? To impress a girl. May I ask who the lucky female Lannybird is?

Urrr, NO, it's for everyone. It's for the whole village and anyone who finds it. It's to make them fall in love with everything. It's my biggest project so far.

Bigger than your Book of Spells?

Same thing really, just outside. And I stole some string, some kindling and plastic sheeting from the garage. Sorreeeeeee . . .

He slithers off somewhere, singing, and I open up my horrid book and type and type and type and type and realise with a strange mix of befuddlement and joy that Lanny is my muse.

LANNY'S DAD

Lanny woke up crying about some ghost story Pete had told him about crooks in the woods.

What the hell is that man putting in his head? I asked her.

Yup, I much prefer your approach of plonking him in front of the TV and checking your emails.

What?

Nothing, go to sleep.

This is how it's been for a while now; magical Pete, mundane Dad.

Truth is, they're right.

I went down there on Saturday to bring Lanny home for lunch and we got talking, old Pete and me. He was painting lengths of MDF so I offered to help, while Lanny was drawing a huge minotaur on a sheet taped to the floor, and we chatted about this and that, and he showed me how to get a good smooth finish on the boards, and he hummed, and we took it in turns to wipe down the side of the boards for drips with a rag, and an hour passed and she came down to get us, asking why we'd missed lunch, and Pete put a loaf and a lump of cheddar out, and we ate, and Lanny brought his giant beast to life with occasional steers from Pete, and then we left, and we chatted with Peggy for ten minutes about the likelihood that the fly-tipper who's been dumping sofas up at Harley Lane would be prosecuted, and only after getting home and opening a beer did I realise it was the nicest few hours of my life for ages, and I hadn't thought about work, I hadn't checked my phone, and I'd enjoyed the painting, and then at some point that afternoon she and I snuck upstairs for a proper long bonk, a giggly natural no-stress romp, and life in the village felt good.

LANNY'S MUM

I was depressed, when we moved here. I'd been ill after Lanny was born and those feelings came back to me. Empty, shrunken, hunted. I had horrifying dreams. I felt watched the whole time, judged, and even when I walked out into the fields and woods I felt scrutinised. And then I cursed the naïvety of the Londoner moving to the country expecting to find there or in themselves ready-made tranquillity.

The first thing I discovered was that the village was noisy. Noisy birds, noisy school playground, noisy farm machinery, endless knocks on the door, all-hours banging and hammering. In the first months I used to go and sit on a bench overlooking the meadow, feeling frightened, and wait for Lanny to come out of school and show me how to live. And once or twice we had prank calls. Well, someone phoned me. When Robert was at work, always when I was alone in the house, the phone would ring and I'd answer and there'd be someone silently there. No heavy breathing or nasty words, but there was definitely someone there. There would be some rustling sometimes, movement, a sense of someone there not saying anything, but I was certain it was someone who knew I was alone in the house. I didn't tell Robert because he was having a lot of midnight freak-outs, checking the doors and thinking that people were peering in at him. He was adjusting. It did occur to me that it might have been him, phoning from work, stalking his own wife from the carpeted hallways of the city. Anyway, it stopped. Perhaps I wasn't playing scared housewife with enough aplomb.

One morning I heard a little scream. A pained noise. Animal rasping. I couldn't tell where it was coming from. I didn't know what to do. I felt I needed a rural life-advice number I could call: Hello, there is tiny screaming, there is small beast whining, and I am a depressed out-of-work actress and my husband is a city slicker who wouldn't know a cow from a boar.

It was a hedgehog caught in the drain. I couldn't
understand how it had got in there. It was distressed.
It was dying. I couldn't see how to get the drain
lid off. There was no way to get it out. I thought I
should shoot it, to put it out of its misery, but of
course I didn't have a gun. I wondered about calling
the RSPCA but I thought they'd laugh at me, for a
trapped hedgehog, when there are stolen dogs and
wounded hawks, when there are foxes being hunted
on an industrial scale by frothing landowning maniacs
around here, my top-echelon neighbours in jodhpurs. I
thought perhaps I should put something poisonous in
the drain, wait for it to die, then rot, then disappear, but
what is a hedgehog poison? And how would I convince
the yelping hedgehog to eat it? I sat in the loo and I
cried. When I came out it had stopped screaming.

Some kind of lethal autopilot took over. I put on my
rubber gloves and got a carving knife. I went out, knelt
over the drain and stabbed the hedgehog several times
in the body and head, trying not to look, attempting
not to breathe too deeply. I kept on going. I stabbed and
sawed through the gaps in the drain cover until the
hedgehog was a pulpy mess of blood and spines, little
bones and shiny bits of pink and white. I kept on going,
I rhythmically chopped and poked at the hedgehog
until it seemed likely that I could rinse it away. I put
the knife and the gloves in the bin, boiled the kettle

and poured the water in. I remembered passing the abattoir in the small town where I grew up, where blood-pink water would run down the street marbled with occasional shocking crimson. I rescued the knife from the bin and mashed the hedgehog a bit more, and then tried another kettle of water. It took two more kettles and ten more minutes jabbing through the drain to erase all trace of the thing. It was gone.

Now how do you feel? I asked myself.

I felt good.

I felt capable, competent and clear-minded. I bleached the sink, washed the knife and returned it to the drawer. You and I have a little secret now, I said to the blade.

DEAD PAPA TOOTHWORT

He was crouched in the septic tank watching this
and he found it very pleasing. He saw in it an aspect
of himself, of his part in things. He watched the
boy's mum mashing a hedgehog, turning panic-
stricken animal into watery blood-spike soup, and he
loved it very much, same as Mrs Larton stamping on
a poisoned mouse to finish it off, same as John and
Oliver shooting jackdaws at the tip, same as Jean
drowning wasps in her jam-trap. One day as good as
any in the human war against others. He loved the
foot-and-mouth culls and spent those months slipping
in and out of burning livestock; nothing new to
Toothwort, veteran witness of the bovine burcs, the
flus, the wonderful rinderpest, rain rot and sheep
scab, the cycles of mange, mastitis and pox, he's seen
things die in thousands of ways,
                                        bit of spindle,
septic splinter, dropped stitch, dieback won by the 90s,   *Red Bull burps,*
I beg you don't sign outside the box or I'll have to start all over again,
          those books where you choose your own ending,
                 sharp debris,   *one in The Bell before quiz* *bang wallop,*
      culling isn't the answer, speak English you prick,
it's a marriage built on lies,   *same ten ghosts, slowly poisoned by toxic yew,*
                         Dad's Taxis at your service,
   nothing says cheapskate or bell-end like a yellow beamer motorsport,
   contaminated water, murderously cold in the garage, *so delicious to see you duck,*

64

Rottweiler pups, *50p each or a strip for £2,*
yes I'm threatening you son,

**He loves it when a lamb gets stuck being
born, when man and ewe and lamb are all suspended,
reckoning with the terrible joke of the flesh and the
rubbery links between life and death,**

all wild things fear the smell of human beings,
Nobody wants a by-election, came home stinking of fags, mysterious footsteps,
god knows what goes on, moonlight sonata and a cigar, Jean Coombe
was hurt as a child,
jab clinic over-booked, while you snooze he nicks your shoes,
coming for our jobs, wicketkeeper first and a barrister second,
laugh my pockmarked arse off, her carrot and coriander soup was the star
of Lenten lunch,
foot-deep in rotten animal bones, nobody says that word any more Dad,
let him know there's danger,
if you could just peel it back and let me get a peek at the sore bit,
nine beers three shots, his you-know-what smelt of a wheelie bin,
choke on hawthorn haws, *ruthless pruning,* *past his* *bedtime*

**Dead Papa Toothwort has seen monks executed on
this land, seen witches drowned, seen industrial
slaughter of animals, seen men beat each other
senseless, seen bodies abused and violated, seen
people hurt their closest, harm themselves, plot and
worry or panic and rage, and the same can be said of
the earth. He has seen the land itself cut apart, its
top layer disembowelled, stripped and re-plundered,**

sliced into tinier pieces by wire, hedges and law. He has seen it poisoned by chemicals. He has seen it outlive its surgeons, worshippers and attackers. It holds firm and survives the village again and again and he loves it. He wouldn't do well in a wilderness.

PETE

She asked if I could do her a favour. If I could pick him up after school from his mate Alfie's house on Chalkpit Lane. Robert was away on business, trebling invisible fortunes or whatever it is he does.

Alfie's mum Charlotte is one of those health and safety types and regards me as smelly and dangerous. She's surely googled me and knows I was once famous for filling a gallery with painted wooden dicks. Her life insurance policy is probably more expensive due to the dangerous proximity of creativity to her neat detached house with underfloor heating and wipe-clean walls.

No offence intended, Peter, she said, not inviting me in, but I think I should just check with Lanny's mother.

She's in London meeting with her publisher, I said. I am instructed to feed Lanny and drop him home at bedtime when his father will be home.

I'm sure that's right, Peter, but let's check shall we?

Yes *let's*, I said.

I shan't lie, I developed a powerful dislike of Charlotte in the time it took for her to go and phone Lanny's mum, and then bring Lanny to the door, *coat/shoes/ rucksack/see y'Alfie/see ya Lanny*, not because of her security measures but because of the framed Renoir reproduction she had in the hallway.

I can usually see a way to understand terrible things; Satanic worship, decaffeinated coffee, cosmetic surgery, but Renoir's portrait of Madame de Bonnières? No. It cannot be understood or forgiven. And framed in gold plastic and spot-lit from above? No offence intended, *Charlotte*, there is not a chamber of hell hot enough for a woman of your taste.

Later we are polishing off jacket spuds with cheese and beans, talking about trees. We agree, Lanny and I, on the beech. An English totem.

I've got a tree book, he says, and I looked up copper beech, *Fagus sylvatica*, and it said 'Grossly overplanted.'

I think I know the book you're talking about. The Collins glovebox thing with the snooty tone. Yup, I have that book. Ignore him. Highfalutin bollocks.

Highfalutin bollocks.

Best keep that to yourself, boy.

Pete?

Yes, sire.

Do you believe in Dead Papa Toothwort?

Eh?

Do you think he's real?

Well, no. Well yes inasmuch as he's real if people believe in him. So yes. Just as mermaids or Spring-heeled Jack or the Green Children of Woolpit are real if people have thought about them, told stories about them. He's a part of this village and has been for hundreds of years, whether he's real or not. You should ask old Peg, she's the expert.

Yeah but Wilf's brother Hugo says he's seen him climbing over their garden fence. A man made entirely of ivy.

I'd take that with a pinch of salt, Lanny.

He swings his legs and chants:

Say Your Prayers and Be Good Too, Or Dead Papa Toothwort Is Coming for You. He lives in the woods. I believe in him. I've seen him.

I change the subject.

I'll tell you something interesting that you may already know from your reading. The bit of a tree that draws up nutrients, the most vital living part of a tree, is actually just under the surface. So a skin wound, a

minor whack with an axe or an arrow or a chainsaw,
can do a lot of damage to a tree, to its living operations.
It grows around that damage.

I know what you're going to say, replies Lanny.

You do, do you?

He stands up and stretches to the ceiling, ribs and tum,
reaching like a sweet pea for the sun.

That humans are just the same.

LANNY'S MUM

I'm woken by sobbing outside the bedroom. Robert
is splayed across the bed like a dead tennis player,
drooling. I go out to find Lanny sitting cross-legged at
the top of the stairs and he can hardly catch his breath
he's so upset.

I hold him and soothe him and he's all warm bumps.
Warm bump of an elbow, of a knee, hot little heels like
pebbles warmed by their own internal sun.

He eventually tells me in gulping whispers that the
little boy in the water charity leaflet will probably
already be dead.

I've wasted so much water, in my baths, running it cold
to drink, watering the garden.

But darling we've talked about this so often, you cannot fix the way the world is broken all on your own. You can't get the water from our tap to that little boy in Africa.

He looks at me like I've said the most grotesque thing ever uttered. He climbs off my lap. His face is darkened with disdain.

Night, Mum.

In the morning he's not in his bed, and there's no sign that he has had one of his early breakfasts and dashed for the woods.

Lanny?

Lanny?

There's a scuffling sound from my office. I find him hurriedly trying to close down my computer. Never has a child looked shiftier in the history of the world.

He turns to me and takes a deep breath. This will be interesting, I think, because Lanny is not a fibber.

I was reading your book.

Oh darling it's absolutely not appropriate. That's a very naughty thing to do. You are far, far too young to read that. It's an adult crime book.

I know. I skipped over the first bit and then skipped . . .
um . . .

Violent. It's very violent.

I think I'm too young to understand it.

I think so.

Shall I read it when I'm a teenager?

Eighteen, I think.

Sorry Mum.

That's OK. I'm sorry about what I said in the night,
about the water leaflet boy.

That's OK. I know what you mean.

I go over, kneel and hug him, and over his shoulder I
read the terrible paragraphs of my unholy novel. I feel
horrible that he has found it. It is not for him.

Mum?

Yes, love?

Because Dad's parents are dead do you think he loves
us more? Do you think he gives us the spare love he
would normally give his mum and dad? Is there extra
love for us?

No, I think.

Yes, I say. That's exactly right.

LANNY'S DAD

A plan has been agreed on. Pete will take Lanny to London to see his exhibition being put up on Cork Street, have lunch, drop into the National Gallery, and be back in time for tea.

I am of course fine with it, and keep being reprimanded by her for speaking with artificial regularity about *how* fine I am with it. And I am. It's fine. I trust Pete and I know Lanny will have fun and be well behaved, and his schoolteacher has already commented on the revolution in his work, the transformation in the way he expresses himself. So it's all good. They asked to get a lift to the station with me but the timings don't work. That's fine too. The idea of Pete in my car somehow embarrasses me. My leather seats.

I don't know who I have to please. I have to please the village but I can't because the village is a place defined for me by its proximity to London and I am therefore part of the problem, cause and effect, my only right to be here is the right brokered for me by a mortgage lender in Canary Wharf so I cling to little victories, little roots and shoots of belonging, believing that my right to be here is Lanny, the well-liked eccentric, my right to be here is my offering to cut Mrs Larton's wisteria, is Pete giving me a beer, is the brick-shithouse builder saying 'cheers mate' when

73

I held open the pub door. I chat to Peggy at least twice a week and Peggy seems to like me, is that not official acceptance?

PETE

She dropped him down, which was unusual as he'd been coming whenever he fancied it, popping in and out. She sent him into the garden and sat down opposite me. She was stern. She asked if I could stop telling Lanny frightening things, ghost stories and such. She said, Robert asks, well, we ask, well, Robert asks. You know, he's only little.

I said, I hate to break it to you, but Lanny's the one telling *me* frightening things.

I know, she said. But the school tell us he's been writing the strangest stories, dark stuff, and behaving a bit oddly, and a girl in year 5 complained he'd put a spell on her.

Ha!

It's not funny, Pete.

I know, I'm sorry. But come on, Lanny's good. Different, and bloody wonderful. If some stuck-up little cow thinks he's a wizard, then so be it. She can give him a bad review on classmate dot com. Really though, a pox on every test and standard and criteria of normality that Lanny will flummox in his long and glorious lifetime. No?

She laughed and put her nice face in her hands.

Well, thanks a bunch for your help, Mad Pete, I'm glad we had this chat.

She got up, patted my shoulder and took her leave.

So that afternoon I strenuously avoided ghost stories and focused on teaching.

He took very well to watercolour painting. Very well indeed. I can't much be arsed with watercolour but Lanny had a good feeling for it. Could guess at absorption and pigment's unpredictability in ways that impressed me, knew without instruction how to use the brush for taking away as well as putting on. You can lick that, I said, if you're in a hurry, suck it clean if you need to quickly undo, doesn't taste bad. But not that lead white, that white's poison.

He looked at the little tube.

How much white would you need to eat to die?

Not a question I can answer, Lanny. A shit ton. There'd be quicker ways to kill a person. Just don't lick the brush when you've got white on it and we'll all avoid prison. Good lad.

We wandered out to paint the lightning tree on the other side of Dogrose Common. He traipsed along, his backpack jangling with water pot, binoculars, snack bar and carton of Ribena. We chatted about football cards and the little plastic fighters he's swapped with his mate and the general Lanny-esque stream of conversation flowed forth, philosophical mutterings and bits of tune all mixed up with standard child babble and suddenly I smelt spliff, sticky rich and green over the airwaves. Lovely smell. In the bus shelter as we passed there was the Henderson boy with Oscar whatsisname from Yew Tree Cottage and they were passing back and forth a joint as big as a church candle, a floppy, knuckled, badly-built thing, and my word it smelled nice. We nodded as we passed and I raised a hand in greeting.

WEIRDO coughed one of them, spluttering into giggles.

We walked on.

I was a little stuck for what to say and then Lanny asked, Do you think they were talking about me or you?

And I shrieked with laughter then, because for some reason I found that stupendously funny and Lanny was saying, What? What's so funny?

We trampled down the dog-walk path towards Hatchett Wood and it was ever so beautiful. The thick wall of green between the common and the wood bursting with life, clematis clambering through and over it, a properly paintable riot, the yarrow glowing a bit, the blackthorn and maple all hugged up together, foxgloves leaning out like thin beckoning arms and I was still wiping tears of laughter from my eyes and considering how surprising it was, me, an old man, tail-end of a good career but a mainly lonely life, finding such a good friend in this little kid.

LANNY'S MUM

We went to the maze at Carlton Hall for a walk and a picnic and to get some use out of our expensive membership card.

Robert was banging on and on about having met Lanny and Pete for lunch in London, about how good Pete looked in a suit.

Properly good, like a trendy old dude.

Darling, he *is* a trendy old dude.

Yeah but he dresses like a scarecrow most of the time. I'm serious, he looked like he ran an ad agency, brown suede boots, lovely linen suit, beard trimmed, tortoise-shell glasses.

Jesus, Robert, you got the hots for Pete or what?

I'm just saying, I think we forget that Pete is quite a big deal. There's books on him. I think he's probably rich.

You are a ridiculous person, Robert Lloyd.

We gaze at the sign, which warns of the maze's difficulty and suggests it takes forty minutes to reach the centre, where there is a walkway and a statue of the Carlton Green Giant.

Where's Lanny?

He was right here.

Lanny?

There's a distant whistle from the maze. We step back outside the first hedge and there is Lanny, on the raised platform in the middle, waving from next to the statue.

What the fuck? says Robert.

We look at each other.

Lanny! Come back. Come back and get us.

We wait. Robert's mouth hangs open as he stares at the maze entrance.

Has he cheated? Did he find a map? Or follow someone? We've been here once before, last spring. He can't have remembered. Nobody could have.

I don't get it.

A few minutes later Lanny bolts out of the maze pink and grinning.

Darling, how did you get there so quickly?

What do you mean?

The middle. It takes forty minutes. How did you get there so quickly?

I ran.

Robert kneels down.

Lanny, how did you know which way to go, I mean, is there a route marked on the floor? How did you get to the centre?

I just ran.

Lanny! Robert holds his shoulders.

Hey, Robert, calm down. Lanny? Tell us the truth,

because it's just really amazing and a bit strange, that's all. How did you know which way to go?

Lanny is completely perplexed, as true and easy as he always is.

I just jogged along. I got to a corner and every time it seemed obvious. Left! Right! I could feel which way to go. I just knew. And guess what! That statue in the middle is Dead Papa Toothwort.

We go and eat our picnic on the hill and Lanny is chatty and Robert and I don't say much.

In bed that night Robert turns to me and asks if I'm still thinking about it.

Of course I am. I don't know what to think.

Love, it's properly strange. It's a freak event. Or he's some kind of number genius who can see things we can't. Weird shit like this, I just, I wonder if we should . . .

Do you remember that time at my parents'?

Please don't, I can't handle it.

I'm referring to a time when Lanny was a baby. He could crawl but not walk. We were in my parents' garden and he suddenly wasn't there. We searched and shouted and started to panic and then we heard him gurgling and giggling and he was in my old tree house at the bottom of their garden. Nine feet up a ladder. Every one of us insisted we hadn't put him there, and we knew we hadn't because we'd all been sat at the table drinking and eating. But we told ourselves afterwards that my dad had done it, he's a joker, he must've crept off and lifted Lanny up there. It was easier to accept that Dad was lying than it was to have no rational explanation.

We lie there in silence.

I am thinking of my baby lying next door asleep. Or possibly he's not asleep. Possibly he's dancing in the garden with the elves or the goblins. We assume he's asleep like a normal child, but he's not a normal child, he is Lanny Greentree, our little mystery.

PETE

Lanny and I are trooping up to his place after I've let him cut some lino and shown him Bellini's *Doge* which rightly knocked his socks off. Said I'd walk him home because I've not been out, and I think I might stop in at the pub for a pint or three and a bag of dry roasted.

We haven't seen so much of each other recently. I've been getting on with new work. He probably doesn't want to hang out with an old man all the time. I was chuffed when he dropped in this evening.

Bellini's *Doge* or Mantegna's *Dead Christ*?

Doge.

Bellini's *Doge* or the upside-down toilet?

Doge Doge Doge. It's the best thing I've ever seen.

Well I'm glad. I agree it's a bit special. I've got a postcard of him somewhere, I'll dig it out. Oh hello, magnetic pensioner at twelve o'clock, Peggy straight ahead, there's no avoiding her, oh boy we're done for, eye contact has been established, she's got us, none can resist her powerful drag, we will have to stop and talk.

No problem, he says, the sociable little bastard.

We find Peggy in mournful mode, which is increasingly the case. Gone are the titbits of village gossip, the exhaustive updates on the state of every marriage. Peggy is these days fairly sad. She's frail, and her bones hurt. She's convinced of a great and unstoppable badness at work in the world. She's not wrong.

What I will say, she says, holding Lanny's hands in the wrinkled cup of her own, what I will say is that it brings me great joy to see you, young man. Everyone marching about on their telephones, speeding about in these huge shiny cars, and you seem to me a child of the old times, a proper human child.

Oh don't be fooled, Peggy, this one knows his way about a computer, he'll be running the show one of these days.

Lanny grins, escapes from Peggy's wrinkly grasp, and ducks from my swipe.

What I will say is that very soon, little man, I will die. I'm the last. I waved my brothers off to war from this gate. They didn't come back, but the village has filled again and again like a rock pool. All sorts. That Mrs Larton likes to pretend she's been here forever, but it seems to me just yesterday that she arrived with her brass-buttoned husband, rosy of cheek, plugged into a bottle of claret all day every day, and she started bossing us all about. They come and go. I see it all. But you're a delight, little man, and you've had a pleasing effect on the place.

Do you know, she says, that I will die and this Victorian cottage will be knocked down, and on this site they will build three *pretend* Victorian cottages. This gate will be replaced by a new gate, faked to replicate this gate's charms.

How do you know? asks Lanny.

I just know.

I won't let them.

Do you know, she says, what the Domesday Book has to say about this place?

No, we both reply in dutiful unison.

It says the bishop holds this place. It says it answers for ten hides, land for sixteen ploughs, twenty-nine villagers and five slaves.

Slaves? I ask, because that doesn't sound right.

Peggy tuts, Slaves just meant folk with no land, Peter.

Oh, OK.

Five slaves, meadows for sixteen ploughs, two hundred pigs, the land valued at eleven pounds.

Eleven pounds, says Lanny, hopping on the spot, I've got twenty-nine pounds in my savings. I could buy it!

Buy it, lad, I say.

Buy it and take good care of it, young man, says Peggy.

Do you know what else it says there in the book?

Peggy leans on the gate with her elbows and takes up

Lanny's hands again and stares into his eyes.

It says, in small letters at the end of the entry, hardly legible but I've seen a photograph copy of it, *Puer Toothwort.*

Oh Peggy, I tut, you rotter, what a load of old bollocks.

It says it, Peter. It was written. He's been here as long as there has *been* a here. He was young once, when this island was freshly formed. Nobody was truly born here, apart from him.

So he's older than you? Surely not. Right then, must deliver this little artist home to his parents.

Night night, Peggy, sweet dreams, sings Lanny.

Sleep well good child, she says. Sleep well, Mad Pete, and she winks.

LANNY'S MUM

He's been very distant. Or I've been very distracted. He comes and goes and seems worried. I can never find him. Tonight I looked for him everywhere and found him eventually floating in a deep bath with only his perfect face emerging from the bubbles.

He is all clean hair and freckles.

You delicious boy. I could eat you.

That would be 'Not OK', Mum.

Mums have special permission to eat their sons, it's a rule as old as time.

Mum? He sits up, dripping.

Yes, love?

Last night I dreamt I went running with the deer again.

Ooh lovely, your favourite dream.

But this time I wasn't a boy, running with deer. I was a deer, inside a deer looking at me, wondering if I was an animal. My bones felt lower and stronger, springy, my eyes were deer's eyes, but I could see me inside the deer and I thought 'a human boy!' and I was excited and really, really worried at the same time. There was a bang and I was pulled backwards, caught in barbed wire or metal teeth or something, and my leg was ripped up and the bone was showing through. The deer were all watching me and couldn't help because they were deer, and I was dying, and they felt terrible because they had tripped me. I knew they'd tripped me and they showed me with their eyes that they had done it because I was human, because they couldn't have a human running as a deer, it wasn't possible. I'd broken the rules. It went on for ages. I needed hospitals and medicine and words and they didn't have any of it so I lay there and waited. I just waited and waited and the deer watched.

Shit, Lanny, darling. What a horrible dream.

Wasn't horrible. Just sad. I felt so sad. What happens when we die?

Why?

Just wondering.

Well, I think our bodies rot and our souls go to heaven. If we've been good.

Do you believe in heaven?

I do, sort of. Yes.

I agree with Pete.

Oh yeah, what does Pete think happens?

He thinks our souls split off and wander around for a bit, seeing things properly. He thinks we see for the first time how things really work, how close we are to plants, how everything is connected, and we get it, finally, but only for a second. We see shapes and patterns and it's incredibly beautiful like the best art ever, with maths and science and music and feelings all at once, the whole of everything. And then we just dissolve and become air.

That's very nice. I'm pleased with that as a thing to look forward to.

Me too.

I love you Lanny.

I know you do.

DEAD PAPA TOOTHWORT

He sits gorged in his favourite stile, wearing a
worried knot for a face,

a so-called mini-break, murderous temper,
        inexplicably drank antifreeze, we warned them,
nice slow shag and a lie-in, colour like dead-for-three-days green,
    what will kill Sandy Cleverdon is old-fashioned laziness
fairly short odds,
        burned alive,
            unhealthy intentions,
                rotting logs,
                    fractured jaw and minor bruising,

Dead Papa Toothwort knows himself, and he
has felt the tightening-itch, and now is the time,

blinding yellow oilseed rape, hunt for the runt or the runt will grow
        so we hunt for the runt with a bow, no breathing room,
dazing, city habit,
        funny little fella, but is it any wonder, hit and run,
a whole basket of dead robins,
                    party, garden waste

he crawls towards the living, climbs
under Spring Lane and washes along so he can come
right up under the village street, so he can float
belly-up under them and sip the bath water and shit,
fat-clumps and grit, a dark attentive voyeur,

        bell-ringing practice moves to 5.30 pm,
        nothing much mate
nothing much mate usual bollocks, locked out of his own life,
        night horrors again poor lamb, sour-breath,

    play Lord I just can't keep from crying sometimes,   89

we told her to be grateful, random acts of aggression doomy forecast,
shitty day that spells, guttering, just the air in the pipes,
border disaster, damp patch,
                                        denied her disability allowance,
    spooked,   badger path,
        bleeding scabs,

                        up into the sinks, shower-
heads and toilet bowls, he allows himself some
intruding, some peeping, some tasting,

        mouldy turnips and swedes,
            properly freaked out on the walk home,
    fox blood,
    fox blood,   won't smoke squalids only green,
        hazel seemed to shrink,   human bones in the walls, the walls,
    he's a heathen, this is our land, had no Wasp-Eze,
                    this is our land,

    every hundred years or so it gets like this, he
can't resist, he feels it coming, he needs to act,

            proper towing chain,
        deathwatch beetles clicking in the beams,
        left out so it soured, suspect behaviour, oily grin,
    vicious   something not right,
    vicious cycle of unfairness,   nothing doing,
                                        nothing doing,

    every now and then he does it, puts on a show,
intervenes, changes the nature of the place,

            stack of old homemade jazz-mags,
        three courses and house wine,

90

dare I suggest he get an effing job and vacate that bar stool,

myths exist for a reason,

burn it, something's off,

we will begin with Psalm 37,

most precious possession,

a nation of rotten souls

sobbing in the bus shelter,

sleep paralysis, ten of us in Stevie's Corsa,

**he can't resist and never could, he can't resist and
never should,**

shall we say eco-conservative and worry about the logo another time,

night my love, dark times,

cola bottles and flying saucers,

fright of my life, mouldy blinds shake, torn ligament,

boys will be boys, clogged up with old hair,

an Englishman has to hunt or be hunted,

frightened pets,

face like a bag of melted anus mate,

godless ferret-handling maniac

shame on them all,

kids have sick ideas,   burning scrub,

people are weird alright,

I got the strangest feeling I was being watched,

he is up to something.

LANNY'S DAD

I wake up fists clenched and buzzing, certain of someone downstairs. Someone in the house. I used to get this a lot, but I'm more accustomed to the sound of the village now. I know a hedgehog making his way along the planted borders, I know the postman's early footsteps on the gravel. I know the alien hum of Mrs Larton's late-night tumble-drying. This isn't that. This is a human body moving.

There is someone in my house.

I don't wake her. I get the cricket bat from the wardrobe and the little bones in my feet crack as I tiptoe out of the bedroom.

My pulse is loud in my ears as I creep across the landing and pause, listening, at the top of the stairs. Nothing but my thump thump thump.

Gingerly down the stairs. Nothing. The words in my brain from the script of terrified male homeowner, 'come on then, you fucking fuck' and the bladder-squirm because I have no actual defensive power, I am not brave, I do not fight, have never fought, I work in asset management and only fight in subtle ways on Microsoft Outlook. I'm terrified.

There's nobody in the kitchen but it shits me up being in there, imagining someone looking in, loads of

them, lines and lines of men with hessian faces, with
razor wire and acid, farmers by day killers by night,
invisible just beyond the window pane watching one
of their number stalk me through this house, Jesus,
it scares and humiliates me so I start to swagger a
bit, performing the 'just looking' in case I am being
watched, how daft, to be worried about what people
think even as I genuinely think there's an intruder
in my home. Nobody in the hallway, nobody in
the lounge, no axe between my shoulder-blades, no
shotgun pointed to the back of my head, behind me
just the corners of my house, in front of me just a
dark interior designed by my stylish wife, my own
reflection, and I fling open the under-stairs cupboard
and feel a proper chest pain, an angina-spasm of dread
and then there is a tight squawk from upstairs –

Robert!

I run up, three steps at a time, imagining – with
absolute conviction and clarity – that there is a big
man in a dark cloak in my bedroom and he has a knife
against my wife's throat, and I stride in, bat raised, and
she is sitting up in bed.

I heard something.

Me too. I can't find anything.

My ballsy woman, she looks fucking terrified. She
whispers.

In *here*. There's someone in here. There's something in the room.

I run over, bat in hand, and I jump into bed beside her, suddenly childlike and not brave at all. I think of newspapers printing photos of our bloodstained walls. My heart is whumping in my chest. Is he in the wardrobe, is he made of the sheets, is he in the ceiling, is he in my wife's skin, is she hiding him, can I kill a person, will it hurt, will he torture us –

I'm frightened,

I'm fr—

A rustle and movement, right here, right with us, under the bed. There's a man under our bed, in our bedroom. We're going to be killed in our beds.

She is gripping my hand as hard as she gripped it when our son came ripping his way into the world.

I need to do this. Maybe it's a lost cat or a frightened refugee or a dying fox or a robed poltergeist. I need to do this quickly and surprise myself with bravery, so without too much pause, curiously calmed by the recognition that she needs me, that I'm caring for her, I swing out of the bed. I roll out and land on the floor with a thump and raise my arm ready to swipe the bat hard across the carpet, ready to smash my bat again and again into the face of the man.

Under the bed, eyes wide open, possibly asleep, possibly awake, is Lanny. Lying stiff and long like a rolled-up rug with his arms by his side, under our bed, gazing beyond me. Our child. No expression whatsoever on his face.

Later, both of us awake and talking it over, she says I was too angry.

You called him a fucking freak.

I know.

You need to apologise tomorrow.

He's grown-up enough to know that he gave us a fright, and I was angry. And he needs to stop doing things like this. It's worrying.

You need to apologise to him.

I know. I'm sorry. I was . . . appalled.

I'm sorry.

I don't think I've ever been more frightened in my whole life.

Shall we spoon?

Please.

PETE

Very strange mood. Drunk a few beers and then some whisky, then some not-ready sloe gin.

The sound in the village was all wrong. I went for my walk around the block and got the ill feeling and hurried back. The darkness was uneven, slippery. I sought refuge in my kitchen but the pressure between different objects in my house was all wrong. Something was bad. I had a glass of drink on the table, a newspaper and a pen, and the three of them were fit to lift off and explode. Things were closing in.

I sat and breathed six in, six out.

On the fridge was a postcard from my friend Ben; a Ravilious, the wonky Westbury horse with the train popping along behind. I've treasured it for years. I looked at this image, this lovely English thing, and I felt sick. Bile in my mouth. Neck sweating like a fever. I grabbed it off the fridge and was going to rip it up, but that didn't seem to satisfy the hatred I felt towards it, which was something long, something accumulated. I necked a load more gin and stared at the postcard. I hated that quaint image. Hatred for this card had seemingly been hiding under the surface of my quiet existence for god knows how long. My whole hateful guilty life queued up ready to land on this poor image.

I loathed it in ways I'd been keeping about my person, in my beard, in my ears, under my fingernails, since my parents told me to sod off because I was a faggot and a disgrace, since I first read those pamphlets about what the brave Englishman did in Bengal, did in Kenya, did in Northern Ireland, since I first watched animals slaughtered, since I first sold my fucking soul to a London gallery, to a glossy magazine, since I first saw supermarket carrier bags in the throats of rotting seabirds, since I saw behind the crematorium curtain to the giggling assistants dropping ash on the floor, this all queued up, these painful things, I don't know what was going on, but I was steaming now. Growling vexed. I got a biro. I sat down and I very carefully drew lines across that postcard. Then I rotated it and drew lines across those lines, a grid to obscure the lush Wiltshire hills, the mysterious Neolithic bullshit, the pleasing clouds, the lovely chuff-chuff two-dimensional train, fuck every lying English watercolour acre before and after it, every moron riding it, and again across, hatching away, tightening the grid, Ravilious disappearing into the dark night again poor man, shiny black ink smudging and denting and obliterating the nice gesture of my friend Ben.

I did not know myself.

I did not know what on earth I was.

LANNY'S MUM

I can't sleep. Robert's breathing sounds like a small door catching the carpet as it opens. Click. Scuff. Somebody enter. Click. Scuff. Somebody leave.

I usually sleep well. The village is tight and muggy tonight.

When I was very unwell, when Lanny was a baby, in London, I read all sorts of things designed to scare young mums. About cot death and crushing, choking and allergies, flat skulls and bent backs, damaged eyes and bad milk. And one night I woke up and Lanny wasn't breathing, and I accepted it. I accepted it easily. It was the middle of the night and I was thirsty and I'd forgotten my lines and the duvet was boiling. I'd been dreaming about that film where the man in the barn pretends to be Jesus. The streetlights were toxic yellow through the curtains and the baby had died.

I lay very still. I didn't touch him. I didn't scream. I didn't move or wonder where Robert was, or panic, or cry. I lay still and I could think clearly. It's over now and you can have your self back, I thought to myself. This tragedy will be the story of your whole life, but it's your life and you can sleep forever and ever if needs be. You've won sleep and lost fear. No more baby.

I remember that night and I strangely cherish it.

Robert farts.

An owl makes half an owl's noise.

I am comfortable in my bed, in this house, in the countryside.

I remember a bit of a prayer or a lyric about passing unharmed through fate's unkind embrace.

DEAD PAPA TOOTHWORT

Dead Papa Toothwort steps up from a brown puddle
and walks through the village dressed like a normal
bloke, flat cap, rain mac and sensible boots, out for
an evening stroll. He whistles his song, and the song
is a set of private instructions. He feeds his plan
into this ordinary home-county place, sliding it like
lubricated wire into the soft flesh of the village, into
buildings, gardens, sewage pipes and water tanks,
up the lane to the big house, round the back to the
sports pitch, into the beer pumps, into the books in
the classrooms, into the gas and electric, into the bell
in the church tower, sucked into nostrils, rubbed into
cotton, into the bodies of men and women, folded
into sweaty creases and scratched into red eyes, into
the dreams of the children and the bones of sleeping
house-beasts, and he whistles and whistles and gives
so much he can hardly hold any idea of himself
together. Exhausting.

He has done this before but never with such
sincerity. He means this terrible thing. He's meant
it forever. He makes a once-in-a-century effort,
whistling his dream into being, setting the village up
for its big moment. By the time he gets to the edge
of the woods he has crumpled into nothing more

than a whiff or a suggestion, he is only silent warm crepuscular danger, and the badgers and owls have seen this before, and they know not to greet him, but to hide.

2

+

+ + +

+

+ +

+ +

+

In came the sound of a song,
warm on his creaturely breath.

Bringing me gifts.

A second or two.

Lanny?

I wonder where he is.

Another second.

Where's Lanny?

The words are still at this stage commonplace, embedded in the normal surface of my day, like Where's the Wi-Fi password sticker? Why is this still itching when I cut the label out? Why are these chicken breasts taking so long to defrost?

Where's my son?

A woman speculates idly about where her child is but doesn't worry because her child is never where she thinks he is.

Such a perfect time of day, look at the time, time to bring in the washing, time to go and get Lanny for his tea, time to myself, time it took me to get up, walk around the house, peer into his room, call his name, water every empty patch of the house with his name, he does this every time, sing-song son-time sounding cheerful, calling Lanny-Bean into the garden, walking whistling Lan-Bun into the street, and if I had known then I would barely have been able to crawl across the road let alone stand admiring the light, if I had known.

But I didn't know.

And I saw myself, as it was beginning. A woman about to be crushed. Beginning to be rebuilt as a model of failure and agony. Of course I knew something was wrong.

Time was straight-faced, ushering, naming me as a principal character. That way, Jolie Lloyd, away from your son.

The woman stands in the middle of a street and yawns and pauses. She is a very good actress. Trained. Such yawning and pausing, it could almost be real.

Stretch and breathe the place, the tarmac, the baking, the cut hawthorn, the scent memory of Fred's ciggie, the wood preservative, the rot, the diesel, some kind of blossom, standing in the street after a day hunched at my screen, looking up the road to see if he might be coming home from his forest camp.

I sent a text message, inviting Robert in. I even hummed softly as I sent the message.

U home normal time? Chicken wrapped in bacon. Roast new pots. Bring wine. Looking for Lanny, as always.

Gaze down the road where he might be with friends, might be detained talking to Peggy or poking around in the pub car park collecting plastic keg caps.

Painfully aware of seconds. Standing, thinking.

over and over and over and over and over and over

*You beauty. Yes, normal time. See your wine order and
reply Already Bloody Got It. Is Lan not at Pete's?*

over and over and over and over and over and over

Nope, Pete's away today. I'll go hunting x

+

I was thinking: Get in. The weekend, my favourite
chicken wrapped in bacon, Jolie in a good mood, nice
weather, Rioja Reserva 2011 in the bag, platform
announced as I glide into the station, a lean mean
commuting machine.

+

A woman walking casually to a neighbour's home,
a barefooted human walking on the road, then onto
spiky gravel then onto pleasingly cool flagstones, a
human being passing from one life to another, surface
by surface. A proper drama now, not a one-woman
show.

I knocked.

I gazed at the six Neighbourhood Watch stickers and
wondered why, when the new stickers arrived each

time, Mrs Larton hadn't unpeeled the old ones. For weight of claim, perhaps. For pride. For proof of historic vigilance. Because she is a dickhead.

+

She knocked. I peered through the spy-glass at her gormless face and wondered why, when Jolie Lloyd had such pretty features, she hid it with that messy hair. For fashionable reasons, I suppose. Or shyness.
To stop her salacious husband seeing her. Because she is foolish.

+

I could hear her wheezing approach, slipper-shuffling down the hallway, hissing and nattering to herself like a fairy-tale witch. I heard her slide the several interior bolts of her Mock Tudor door. She peeked out of the crack and said downwardly, Oh.

+

I could see her waiting out there, twiddling the strands of her mop, biting on her lip and fidgeting like a nervous teenager. I took pleasure in slowly unbolting the door, one lock at a time. I feigned surprise at the sight of her and said cheerfully, Oh!

+

I said, Hello Mrs Larton, have you by any chance seen
. . . and she interrupted,

Are you an educated person?

Excuse me?

Did you go to a good school?

I'm sorry, Mrs Larton, I was just looking for . . . and
she interrupted again,

Because I would have thought that the words 'No
Parking on the Verge' were fairly intelligible, fairly
explicable, to someone with even rudimentary
schooling.

Oh, I'm sorry about that. It was a friend of Robert's
and they moved as soon as you came and rang the bell
and actually, sorry, I wonder if you've seen Lanny?

The little girl?

Um, our son. He's a boy. You know Lanny.

And she slammed the door.

+

I thought to myself, I shall get to the bottom of this
parking kerfuffle, but she interrupted;

Had I seen the little child?

Excuse me?

Had I seen Lanny around?

I'm sorry I said, but I have gone out on a limb to welcome you to our village, and I did especially ask that you don't park on the verge.

She muttered about her flashy husband and his sportscar-driving co-conspirators and tried to change the subject to her peculiar little child.

How rude.

I'm terribly sorry but I'm rather busy, I said.

I politely closed the door.

+

I blushed and felt tears prickling. I dislike confrontation and I was embarrassed. I was outraged. I breathed deeply. Mrs Larton can do this to me. She's done it before. My husband finds it funny that I fear and despise her, that I obsess about her, that she can upset me so much. He jokes that I will murder her. It is one of my husband's privileges to joke about things that upset me, here, in this village that we moved to so he could *not* be here, day after day, this village that we moved to so I could be begging a disgusting old woman to help me, to be a good person for two fucking seconds while I ask her if she's seen my child wandering about this afternoon.

✦

I considered the situation and felt quite virtuous. I jolly well put her in her place and I was pleased to have done so. I was relieved. I pondered her behaviour. They are still new here. They parked on the verge. Her husband treats the village like a place to sleep and recharge his batteries, a model village to show off to his chums from Clapham or whatever god-awful place they came from for fresh air or a good school, and I don't ask for much but I did ask, very politely, if they could not park on the verges as they had been expensively re-turfed, and she turned up at my door as if nothing had happened, I had to *coax* an apology from her, and all she cared about was her wandering waif.

✦

I knelt down and said loudly into the letterbox,

Mrs Larton, have you seen Lanny?

✦

Can you believe she pushed open my letterbox?

To scream abuse at me!

✦

I was childlike in the hot stew of my humiliation and frustration. I wish I had filmed all this on my phone to show Robert. I am going to kill a not-very-well-disguised version of Mrs Larton in my next novel. I was furious.

+

I was quite frankly baffled by this show of impropriety and aggression. I wished there had been someone there to witness this. I was going to need at least two episodes of *Antiques in the Attic* to relax me. I was furious.

+

What if we said what we really felt?

+

What if one said what one really felt?

+

What if we, the too-polite sons and daughters of these old fuckers, actually started picking them up on their warped world-view, on their grotesque self-interest and petty entitlement? What if I did murder Mrs Larton? The world would be a better place. How lovely it would be to kick in her door and ask her again: I just wondered if you'd seen my son, you awful bitch, you pissy clingfilm hag and by the way I hate hate hate you, I despise your smell of fetid carpets and toast; Silk Cut, marmalade, gas and antiques. I feel sick just thinking about your yellow-stained lamb's-ear fuzzy upper lip, your heirloom rings stacked on your Churchillian pug-knuckles, the inside of your huge dank house, your weighty silver biro in your splotched hand as you scratch away at the puzzles in your evil newspaper.

Oh god, you horrible crone, you are the worst thing about living here, you are the worst thing about this English village. You are the worst thing about England. And villages. I wish you would die so somebody nice could move in here.

+

What if we, the generation of people who remember the war, actually told these frightful, entitled young people that this is a country we fought for, that you cannot simply *buy* a sense of belonging on your mobile phone. She might have attacked me, yelling Where is Lanny, as if I had him hidden in the larder. I could have phoned the police. Then she wouldn't come around here banging and shouting about how she's lost track of her moping little gypsy with his daft hair and strange singing. I'd like to tell her about the real community around here, a community that is dead and gone thanks to people like her, buying up the houses and putting in ridiculous open kitchens and glass walls. Of course it is arch-lunacy to expect this young girl with a made-up name to understand any of this, she may as well be a bloody foreigner. I worry about the impact on the community. I worry about standards slipping. I worry about this country. I wish she would get bored and let somebody decent move in.

✝

But I spoke calmly and kindly through the letterbox:

Mrs Larton. I'm sorry that our friend parked on the communal verges. Please, if you see Lanny, could you call me? We'd be very grateful. He hasn't been home this afternoon and it's getting dark. Thank you. OK, bye now.

✝

But she seemed to immediately realise the error of her ways:

Mrs Larton, I'm so grateful for the extraordinary kindness you've shown us. Please, if you see Lanny, could you telephone? We're worried. He hasn't been home after his art lessons. Thank you. You're so kind.

✝

I was halfway down the path when I heard the hinge of the letterbox squeak open. I turned around and saw her little fingertips holding it open from within, and she said two words before it slammed shut. She spat the words out and I imagined them rolling down the path towards me as if escaping her. I almost felt I could pick the words up, wipe them clean of her tarry spittle and put them in my pocket.

+

Mad Pete.

+

She was shuffling away down the path but I felt I couldn't not state the very obvious. I waited until she'd turned around and spoke through the letterbox, telling her where I thought the child was. She was utterly unresponsive, as if the words I'd said had been a little delayed in reaching her. I almost felt I could have walked to her, overtaking my words, and said the name right into her strange head:

+

Mad Pete.

+

And then the word Lanny started bursting like

blossom on the branch of the evening. The word Lanny rising up aberrant and abnormal.

Hi, it's Jolie, have you seen Lanny?

✦

Archie, is Lanny up there with you?

✦

Theo, have you seen Lanny since school?

✦

It's Lanny's mum, she's asking if we've seen Lanny.

✦

Jolie's texted asking if we've seen Lanny.

✦

Give Peggy a knock, ask if she's seen Lanny would you?

✦

That's Lanny's mum asking if we've seen Lanny. He's not with his old boyfriend apparently.

✦

She apologised for phoning me at home. I said don't worry. It was 7.50 and I had just put our plates in to soak.

I said Lanny left school as normal, spring in his step, only difference is that he took his sports trainers with him. I distinctly remember seeing he had his little trainer bag.

I said he's presumably at Pete's having his art classes and she said nope Pete's in London today.

+

Panicky call from Fitty McFitterson, the one with the invisible husband, she's lost her weird kid.

+

It's getting dark.

+

And then the word Pete started bursting like blossom on the branch of the evening. The word Pete rising up aberrant and abnormal.

+

Duh, Mad Pete's just tucking him into a shallow grave, LOL.

+

Don't like her, never have. Up her own arse.

+

He answers the call through the car speaker, yes, he's
on his way, yup he'll keep an eye out for Lanny, maybe
drive around the back way in case he's come the long
way home from his camp or something. Yes, he'll
stop at Pete's. Yes, he does think it's odd, but probably
nothing to worry about, thank fuck it's Friday unleash
the chicken wrapped in bacon I am ready, I am ready
for that bastard in my tum-tum.

+

Hi Julie it's Laura, Ben's mum, I just got your
message—

Jolie.

Sorry?

Jolie, not Julie.

Oh, I'm sorry. *Jolie.*

That's OK. You were saying?

Oh, Ben says he saw Lanny this afternoon walking
down the high street after school.

Down?

Yes, as in towards town not the other way.

OK, thanks Laura, that's really kind, I think he's

probably stopped in for tea with a friend and he'll
scamper up any minute. Thanks for calling.

OK, you take care Julie. Oh my god what am I like,
sorry, Jolie!

+

Pete's place is locked up, dark. I peer in. I tap on the
kitchen window. All the weird stones lined up along
Pete's windowsill. Stones with holes in.

Pete?

I wander round the back in case they're in the studio.

Lan-Bean?

Lannster?

Llandudno?

I feel silly. He's not here.

There's a bloody great fibreglass tree stump at the
bottom of Pete's garden. I've always wanted to see if
it's hollow.

I creep across the long grass, stepping over rusted paint
cans and half-built frames, twisted bits of wood, slabs
of rock, tables and ligatures, animal heads and god only
knows what half-built sculptures or junk or both and
I feel sure I'm the first man in a Paul Smith suit ever

to tread this somewhat enchanted ground, and as I get to the tree I feel fairly sure that Lanny is hiding in it and is going to jump out and scare me shitless, so I say, Lanny? And I leap up to the open stump and shout, Got you!

Found you.

He's not in the tree.

Got you.

There's just weeds and junk in the tree. I feel a bit scared. I look back up the garden and feel like Pete's house is watching me. All this old shit and bric-a-brac in Pete's garden has witnessed me making a fool of myself. Witnessed me not finding my son hiding in a fake tree. Of course he's not hiding in the fake tree.

I was thinking: Please, Lanny, don't be annoying. Come home.

✝

Should we call Jolie and see if Lanny's turned up?

It's dark, he'll be home.

Away with the fairies, that boy.

✝

Chicken not in the oven, sitting being the chicken that will never be cooked.

+

Woman stands, as if completely normal, and gazes at her phone.

+

Has Pete ever mentioned a mobile phone?

+

Starting to actually,

Starting to . . . no nothing.

No go on.

Starting to worry.

+

The artist Peter Blythe?

Yes, that's him, could you give us a call if you see him.

+

It was suddenly 10 pm and the rising feeling of sickness was in the house, was in our chests and throats and our arms felt flu-like, our bladders buzzed, our skin tightened because we knew the hours were passing

and they were bad hours, normal evening turning into
really worrying evening turning into terrifying endless
night, no more Jolie, no more Robert, no more family,
no more story, it's ten o-fucking-clock where is Lanny,
the facts are this, he has never stayed out past dark, well
once, but not alone, he isn't with Pete or staying over at
Archie's or Alf's, Robert has walked up Giant's Field, he
has shouted long and hard at the top of the kite-flying
field and if Lanny were in those woods he would not be
naughty enough to not reply, Greg has also done the
loop, shouting, Sally has driven around the village nine
times, has driven into town and back slowly, looking
out for Lanny, he is naughty but not like that, he isn't
naughty, how naughty is Lanny, not a question we ever
ask, he isn't naughty, he isn't hiding from us, where
the hell is he we keep asking what's he doing, what's
he playing at, we said that a lot, play, playing, one of
Lanny's games, one of Lanny's weird tricks.

+

I was thinking clearly. Adrenalin. Jolie's parents are
saying, Why haven't you phoned the police he's a
tiny child he's a small boy what in god's name are
you doing not phoning the police and what in god's
name are you doing both at home, one of you stay
home stay by the phone one of you get out there with
a torch and find the bloody kid, go to his camp, go to

the churchyard, go to the playground, go to the swilly-
swamp, go to the bus shelter, go to the village hall, go
to the pub car park, go to the holly hedge.

+

Got him? And she says, No, come home, the police are
here.

+

come   home

+

It's dark

+

Peggy's stood in the dark at her gate, watching.

+

A lot of people arrive.

+

They're in there searching his house, so let's quit
joking, this is grim.

+

None of us have slept.

+

Bloody sirens and lights, mate, proper bacon in the place.

+

I was looking out of the curtains at the lights and all the people coming and going up and down the street and I said to Gloria: This is what *suddenly* means. A teacher once told me the word suddenly is lazy. And the word nice.

But suddenly, Gloria, this is not nice.

+

This isn't something we are watching on telly. It's just wolfed down a night and a day, nobody knows what time it is, there's a lot of nasty gossip, and all we know is that Pete's been taken in for questioning. Peter Blythe for fuck's sake.

+

There are twenty-three people in my house and a crowd of people in my driveway and many, many cars and vans and a man on the roof with a harness on.

+

Do you want to un-say that, Stuart? There are several hundred people, at this very second, casting aspersions on their parenting. Judging. Telling stories. I don't think you wanna be that person do you?

+

Look at me, Robert. Look at me, man. Look at me. If
he has touched a single hair on that boy's head, I will
dismember him with my bare hands. I will rip the
man's heart out of his chest and stamp on it until it is
part of the floor.

+

It beggars belief that they ever left the kid alone with
him, let alone countless times.

+

I'm looking at poor Jolie's hands, the bloody patchwork
either side of every nail where she has bitten and
chewed her fingers. She is saying, Please, can you
please understand, I don't know any more. Time's
gone mad. Yesterday feels like weeks ago feels like
this morning, it's all bent and confused. I'm sorry. The
policeman tells her not to apologise. I catch Fergus's
eye and we make our excuses and leave them to it,
poor lambs.

+

A helicopter hovers above the village like a fat bee,
hassling the ceiling.

+

Newsflash, there's no such thing as innocent old men hanging out with little children.

+

Going out again. Can't sleep. Me and the boys have drawn a circle with Mad Pete's place in the middle, chucked a brick through his window for good measure. We'll find the kid.

+

She braked suddenly. I was chucked against the seatbelt. She shook her head at me in the wing mirror. I was frightened, to be in a police car.

You understand how serious this is, don't you, Peter?

+

Molested, kidnapped, abused, fiddled, nabbed, abducted, I was just tripping out with the absolute severity of this, could hardly handle it, so a few of us went to the pub and it was rammed with other people, strangers, all just like holy crap some old man has nicked a kid.

+

Pause and breathe, my heartbeat saying time-time time-time, time to put a wash on, time to get Lanny, think hard enough, I can hear him,

howdly-doo Mum, Howdly-hey,

what's for tea, I'm so hungry today.

+

They keep telling me what my rights are, that I can ask
for food if I want it, that I can go to the loo if I need
it. Hideous strip-lighting, my stuff in bags, nobody
allowed to ask me anything until other people arrive
and me saying to every one of them that comes in the
baby-blue sterile room that I would not touch Lanny,
and asking every five minutes What's happened to
Lanny, I've given finger prints and a mouth sample
and my hands have been wiped and they said We don't
need your permission as if I was holding it back and
It will be better if you tell us now, if you tell us right
now, Pete, are you innocent, Pete, am I innocent Pete,
into room five, interview five, train tickets and clothes
and are there people in my house, waiting for the
CCTV from National Rail, from Cork Street, yes there
are sir, there are people in your house and you need to
tell us where the boy is, I think you'll find we can do
whatever we like Mr Blythe, and one of them whispers,
Being near the what? Because they think, you think,
we know, I've done something to Lanny, spit it out
then you miserable jobsworth arsehole, no I do not

want more tea or a lawyer I want to see Jolie or Robert, I want to go home, I want to help find Lanny, and then surprise surprise the local nutbag, what a cliché, and I feel suddenly like I want my mum or my gallerist or Ben or anyone to tell them I'm not a nutbag at all I'm a bloody famous artist, that's hardly the point, no matter, are you, I don't, I could buy this whole police station if I sold a few old bits I've got stored, and I want Lanny to explain to these people, just see it, get me out, just done some reading on you, fairly infamous in the day, bring me Lanny and that's exactly the point, Mr Blythe, you need to tell us where he is, fairly controversial figure, please calm down, did the parents know about your work, the shocking stuff, OK present in the room are, when did you last see the child, tape's going on again, everybody ready, any time you need a cup of tea, Mr Blythe, did we hear from DCI Myerscough, we're on the same side, Pete, can we just get you to move slightly nearer the recorder there, everyone wants the same thing, can we get some water in here please and some tissues, everyone wants little Lanny home safe.

+

He's not hiding in your mobile phone is he, you little city slicker, get out there and look for him. Search for him. Get at it.

+

Soup and prayers. Then more soup and more prayers. My friends; we've been in training for this.

+

Why would his school bag and sports shoes be in your shed?

I imagine he put them there.

Try again.

I imagine he came by and dropped them in there. He has done before. He's free to come and go at my place.

Why did you hide them?

I didn't.

Will you swear in a court of law that you did not place those two bags in your shed?

I will.

Forensics will go a long way, Mr Blythe, to ascertaining whether you are telling us the truth.

I want a cup of tea. This is fucking madness.

Again, language please.

+

She said, It's what we're all thinking, and I said, No it isn't Ellen, no it isn't. It's unthinkable. Don't think it.

+

Every bump in the field looks like a curled-up kid. My stomach is liquid.

+

To clarify, we are looking for a living child. This is a search for a missing child. There is every statistical likelihood that Lanny will come home in the next six hours, cold and apologetic.

+

Edward, if you say anything to me about conspiracy theories or plots I swear to god I will divorce you, just shut up, just shut up for once, or get out there and look for him.

+

Can you describe for the benefit of the tape what we are looking at, some stuff from my studio, can you be more specific, some, please this is ridiculous, please, it's Lanny's name, go on please, it's Lanny's name written down again and again, fifty-five times to be exact Peter, Mr Blythe that is almost obsessive wouldn't you say, it's just a doodle, I do lettercutting, type, it's just an

absent-minded thing, but you must have been thinking
about him while you did it, no, do you mean no you
weren't, no, not like that, perhaps, it looks to me like
a love letter, it might seem to a casual observer that
this is rather obsessive, not at all, can you describe for
the benefit of the tape what we are looking at, if we
could just answer, some stuff from my studio, haven't
slept what time, can you describe for the benefit of the
tape, it's a page from my sketchbook, go on, I don't
understand, you've asked me and I told you I want to
go and help find Lanny, I don't understand, what's on
the page Mr Blythe, it's a drawing of two people having
sex, it's a drawing, not just a drawing is it, there's
probably twenty thousand drawings in my house,
I don't think, I just make work, I've been making
work for decades, some of it's like this, Mr Blythe
I understand that but explain to me the difference
between these 'life drawings' and pornographic
drawings, NO, well Mr Blythe, I shall rephrase that,
these are explicit drawings of androgynous figures
engaging in sex acts, NO, where is the nice lady with
the rose perfume she said I had nothing to worry
about, you'd be advised to calm down, please, NO,
that'll do, we can take a break, I don't like this I want
to wait, hang on, go on, what, go on, I, good god I don't
know how else to explain to you, you think, wait,
Mr Blythe let's take a break, this is not, I know what

you're saying, I've always made work about sex and
always drawn and there's no connection what absolute
madness, hands clammy guilty guilty calm down, what
is this a Victorian indecency trial I am so unhappy I
want to speak to someone else this is just ridiculous
people have written books people have written doctoral
studies on my drawings and Christ alive is this a
serious thing now are you, bloody hell, they're not
the doodles of a sex pest I am, god almighty, I'd like to
speak to someone, so in your art classes with Lanny did
you ever, NO NO NO stop it I can't believe, stop what
Mr Blythe, calm down please, Mr Blythe, every time
he moves his hands there is a sweaty print on the black
plastic table top Mr Blythe?

he lifts his hand

a wet hand remains

there's no difference between their voices and his voice
and the thoughts in his head and he believes he can
hear the thoughts in their heads too

he lifts his hand

he lifts his hand and the cool air of the room washes
away the water and heat of the mark so he places
his other hand down and leaves another print and a
Rorschach-couple more appear, heat prints, stress,
then fade,

and he thinks about ants carrying water droplets
on their backs, tiny water sacks and he remembers
swimming in Greece as a teenager in the weirdly warm
sea and the point on the cliff where the locals had
told him to dive down, he dived down and met a blast
chamber of icy fresh water

a corridor of freezing silence cutting into the hissing
lukewarm salt

diving again and again

every time shocking

like a visitor at the wedding of two warring waters

again and again diving down Blythe down again into
the water Mr Blythe

I'll swear on a bible, on my cousin's life, on every mark
I've ever made on paper, wood or canvas, that I would
never harm that child.

Mr Blythe?

Can you describe for the benefit of the tape what we
are looking at?

   +

Into a van, chloroformed, to Dover, down through
France, Spain, across to Morocco, wakes up the

plaything of a rich pervert with a pomegranate in his mouth. Good night Lorraine I don't want to think about it any more. We don't know.

Well *someone* knows.

✝

All day every day. The second hand of the clock barbed-wired and cutting.

✝

In a word; oblivious. To bullying, to competition, to classroom politics. Off with the fairies. But very sophisticated and intuitive at the same time. He was a joy to teach. Is. Oh dear. Sorry.

✝

I was thinking How should I behave? I went back out but the search teams were so organised and everyone said Go Home Robert You Rest and I was the most hopeless and fraudulent human being.

✝

You keep saying that. Stop repeating yourself and concentrate on what we know.

✝

Julian and Fi's eldest was going to do his dissertation on Peter Blythe, huge fan he was, so he'll have to think again now.

+

The colour of his eyes, but not how he fist-bumps when he's enjoyed a meal. The make and shape of his rucksack, but not the little ridge of freckles across his nose and cheeks.

I've told them.

I've forgotten.

I mentioned it.

I remember.

The colour of his eyes, but not how he sings as he walks. The make and shape of his rucksack, but not the little scar on his knuckle.

+

Silence in the room.

+

That picture of Pete in the seventies, got up in full-on Moondog garb, I mean, you'd do a CRB check on that bastard would you not?

+

She says it again in her velvety-soft professional way:
There's no *accepted* way of reacting.

+

Fame at last: Nan was on the ten o'clock news saying
about how Mad Pete was well dodge.

+

I am speaking, but I don't recognise my own voice. My
voice and all these other voices and the hammering
noise of the fact that he still hasn't turned up.

+

Who is this man in a shiny grey suit with blue plastic
bags on his feet, two iPads and a portable chemistry lab
sitting on Lanny's bed?

+

They should check Peggy's woodshed; she's been
stealing babies since the Middle Ages.

+

There are fifteen people talking at once, busily
translating Lanny into an A4 page of missingness, a
speck in the sea of missing people.

✢

A crucial fixture is a crucial fixture, whatever else might be happening and we will win it for him, for the kid.

✢

All I will say and you didn't hear this from me is that some very odd things were found in his home.

✢

Sleeplessness does the devil's joinery, son.

✢

Someone knows where he is, says Sally for the four hundred and fiftieth time and I will kill her, but she's been a rock. Hasn't Sally been a rock?

Find. My. Son. Swap my husband for my son, take him, get him out of my sight, get everyone out of my sight. I will close my eyes and draw Lanny on the inside of my eyelids in detail only I am capable of and when I open them I want to see him.

✢

Imagine, just imagine being that woman, even for ten minutes, Jesus Christ.

✢

It is one thing and one thing only: negligence.

+

That tea-towel with a cheeky raccoon saying 'Lord grant me patience but please hurry!' I mean how insensitive?

+

Gavin, the Child Abuse Investigation Team (CAIT) Duty Sergeant, says, Talk to Robert. Ask Robert what he's thinking.

+

Think about that, about having *no idea* where your son is, for whole afternoons, whole chunks of days.

+

I was thinking: Let Jolie's dad off his leash, let him murder Pete and bring home Lanny, let him tuck me up in bed, let him patronise, belittle and infantilise me forever and ever in return for Lanny skipping up the driveway saying, What's going on, Dad, what are Gran and Gramzo doing here?

+

I have to ask. Do you *want* Pete to have killed Lanny? Do you want that? Do you want a body?

+

Nice Adam says, They will prioritise DNA testing
when evidence pertains to a missing persons case but
nevertheless the laboratory is in London and just to
be crystal clear Lanny's DNA is all over this village
like magic fairy dust. Just to be clear forensic evidence
of Lanny is everywhere. It is all up and down the
street, behind the hall, around the pub, in more than
a dozen of the houses, into bedrooms and playrooms
and garages, into the woods, onto the common, up the
bloody trees, excuse my language. No problem Nice
Adam carry on please! Well, it's almost as if Lanny's
scent *is* the village's scent and he's staring us in the
face.

+

I've looked in every wheelie bin and every single time,
every lifted lid or bin bag, I have expected to see a dead
child and that's taken its toll and I'm drinking tonight
even though it's a dry day OK?

+

Did I or did I not say they was an odd couple, Jolie and
Rob, well, not to mention Pete and the lad, y'get me.

+

There is no such thing as trust. It's a pernicious myth.

+

I am in the greenhouse. It's a mess. Ambitious vegetable plans abandoned. There are police boot prints in the beds. There is a smashed pot.

The little white flowers are open on the seed potato plants, so I grab one and lift it up. There in the hole, some clinging to the roots, are a dozen perfect baby spuds. And a plastic bag. I kneel down. I wipe the bag on my shirt.

Somehow I intuit that this is important, so I am furtive. I look back at the house, at the people inside my house. I don't want them seeing this.

It's a zip-loc freezer bag. Inside there's a piece of paper with Lanny's writing on it.

I am breathing fast and possible scenarios are tumbling off me like soil off a shaken root.

But it's simpler than that. It's so typical of Lanny; the sweetness, the desire to please, the forward-thinking charm.

'HELLO SEED-POTATO HARVESTER HOORAY FOR TODAY IT'S SEED POTATO DAY!'

I lie down on the scrubby floor of the greenhouse, clutching my boy's letter from one hundred or more days ago, and I weep and grind my knuckles into the ground. I would have found this. I would have called to him. We would have smiled and pulled up the little spuds together, shaking them free.

+

You could give her a hug but she'd bite your arm off.

+

I was thinking: Would Lanny fight or struggle against someone trying to bundle him into a car? Is Lanny going to be sexually assaulted and murdered? Is Jolie having these thoughts? Can I protect her from these thoughts? I know from TV they have corpse dogs who can pick up the smell of dead bodies, these dogs aren't corpse dogs, they're looking for a living Lanny, smelling his funny milky smell, his clothes, his unwashed hair. My thoughts were slippery and grim and I was pretending to be busy.

+

It is very important that you sleep.

I can't.

I can help with that.

If you want to help, get everyone you know, everyone you have ever met, and walk every inch of this country until you find my child then bring him back to me.

+

The unlikeliness of Lanny. Nobody can remember whether he was good at football. He was fine at football. He sang a lot. Really? He sang a lot, but was good at football? He sang, therefore he was mocked. No, not Lanny, he had a kind of magic, we all accepted he was enigmatic and special. A kind of magic, and what, it worked on adults, kids, everyone? I don't believe it.

+

At any time of day, you will find there are twenty-odd rubber-neckers, tragedy tourists, huddled by the plastic tape. Blows my mind. And Angela Arsehole Larton bringing them tea!

+

Someone has sprayed TOOTHWORT TOOK HIM on the bus shelter.

+

Walter started acting funny, barking, sniffing around that weird little concrete pill-box thing by the sledging field, and I thought oh shit, here goes, this is it, I'm going to see a dead body, I'm going to have to carry a dead child a mile home, I'm going to be in the paper, but it was just a decomposing badger, maggots pouring out of his eye sockets like a slow-motion leaderless army, charging, retreating, swirling in confusion.

+

I dreamed of myself as the Virgin, feeding Lanny, a bracelet-wristed European painted baby on my lapis lazuli robes, the village in the background, Robert tiny in the fields gathering hay, and as Lanny fed Lanny grew, he swelled and stretched into a big long muscled man, carved, released from whatever invisible rock the baby was imprisoned in, draped across my lap, bearded, his big knob falling down towards the earth, still feeding, glugging at me, fast asleep but thirsty, and my tits were made of cabbage leaves, and my son was made of marble, and Robert was in the background, tiny, desperately harvesting, kneeling down pulling at hopeless straws, and in the mirror, half obscured, was Pete, painting us.

+

No missing kid is ever annoying or boring are they? 'We won't really miss his plain face or his bog-standard school work. He was unremarkable, a bit of a pain actually, and we're glad he's gone.'

+

Dear Jolie and Robert I am thinking of you. I feel terrible I was sometimes mean to Lanny. Most of the time I wasn't but one time I called him a retard and he might have been upset. I'm really sorry. I think about him and say prayers that he will come home. From James Stead.

+

They offered me a hotel. They advised me not to be in the village. But I want to look for Lanny. Don't provoke people, they said. Feelings run high at times like this. But I want to see Jolie. I want to help my friends. I want to find Lanny. Then a little man who looked like a sleepy vole came and said to me that I would need counselling. He warned me that I might not ever be able to live in the village again. I should see a psychotherapist and take full advantage of the legal, financial and emotional support being offered to me. And I should not talk to newspapers.

Do you believe in God, Mr Blythe?

No, I said.

Just checking, said the sleepy vole. It can come in handy.

+

I knew you were insensitive but I hadn't realised you
were hateful.

+

RAPE, MURDER AND SADISTIC VIOLENCE:
Read scenes from Lanny's mum's 'hotly tipped crime
debut'.

+

Silence please. At the risk of repeating myself, please
do not antagonise the grandpa. Please respect the FLO
and the delicate work she now has to do.

+

He's a sex slave in Saudi Arabia, he's a busker in Fez,
he's in a bag of builder's rubble on the mossy bottom
of Dudley Canal, he's acid, he's sewage, he's concrete,
he's got a new face now.

+

Look me in the eye and tell me it's not exciting, the
whole country watching.

+

I thought he was a right little knob skipping about like
he was a fairy princess, but you shouldn't speak ill of
the dead should you.

+

Pete walked a full loop of the village in bright daylight like he gave absolutely no fucks, fair play to him.

+

No longer a suspect. Has a water-tight alibi from the moment that boy left school to this very second. A Water. Tight. Alibi. Can we just repeat that for the benefit of Captain Witch-hunt over there on the fruit machine?

+

You've never seen anything like this kid's collections. Like Pitt Rivers in his bedroom, fossilised wood and crystals and stones all labelled '40 million years old', 'Suffolk beach', 'Dad's first fool's gold', shark's teeth, worry dolls, knots, finger bowls, acorns, shells, stalactites, wishbones, everything labelled, everything loved.

+

Brave, to come straight back here, look us all in the eye.

+

Dear Mr and Mrs Lloyd, We were in the woods playing BB guns and we found Lanny building his

camp and we called him a weirdo and kicked the
wall and broke a bit and I tripped him up and we all
laughed. I'm so sorry, he was a really cool boy and
I hope he's OK and will be home soon. From Dean
Dawes. PS I'm sorry.

✝

Pam has a library of this shit.

What shit.

You know, missing kids.

Eh?

The murder cases, missing kid mysteries, all those
books about famous dead children.

That's fucked up.

Yeah she told me she's kind of loving this.

That's fucked up.

Yeah she said being this close to the drama is a dream
come true and she sort of hopes it doesn't end.

That's the sickest thing I've ever heard, Fat Pam is
evil.

Yeah man, but you shouldn't call her Fat Pam that's
not cool.

+

May I remind you, Nick, that on day one, DAY. ONE, Jolie said she did not believe Pete would harm her child. She said that on day one.

+

I know you generously did the first 1000 postcards free, but you are the only local business charging for help with the campaign, and you being, you know, Polish and therefore not 'of' the community in the traditional sense, I would hate for word to get out that you were profiting from Mr and Mrs Lloyd's, well, all of our, terrible tragedy.

+

Oi, Paedo, you've got a cheek. Can't fool a fooler. Few of us wouldn't mind a word.

+

Dear all,

I met this morning with Caroline, Jolie Lloyd's editor, and with Martin from the division legal team, and I can confirm that we will pull this novel from the schedule indefinitely. Thank you all for calm heads when the pages were leaked, and for your care and sincerity. I think we can be extremely proud of how we have behaved, as publishers and people, during this terrible time for one of our most promising new writers. With warm wishes,

Susan

+

Bunch of tough guys, attacking an old man. Big men. Flinging punches at a weeping pensioner.

+

Facts are my bread and butter, Agnieszka. Seven hundred *thousand* kids run away every year. About seven hundred kids are snatched every year. Let's allow probability to triumph over blind panic and sinister phantasms shall we?

+

Old posh-pants Howarth hasn't said much, has he? Keeping shtum in case the police find the hundreds of dead prozzies in his garden?

+

Peggy kneels and places her ancient hands on the acorn-garland carvings on the chest her great-grandfather carved out of local oak. She whispers, Look after him.

She waits and she runs her fingertips over the wood.

She sighs. Shooting pains in her knees and up her
spine.

I know you.
I know what you're up to.
Give the boy back.

+

Different dogs, mate, won't smell a living kid.

+

Authenticity competitions, striving to be the one that
most belongs here, guarding their own special spot
in the picture. All this has shown what a bunch of
wankers most people are.

+

His hair, his eyes, his gait, his front teeth, his
ankle socks, his scarred knee, his laugh. You will
know him by the golden fluff on his shins. I
would know him by his milky morning-breath.
Findhimfindhimfindhimfindhim.

+

Jen was refreshing every five minutes, Lanny, #Lanny,
#Lannynews, #findLanny, but unlike Jen I'd actually

been on the news so I was also kind of addicted to
looking out for myself on telly and everyone said I
looked fit. Really sad obviously but also fit.

+

Just to let you know that we are thinking of you every
second of every day and this evening we said a special
group prayer to St Anthony for Lanny's safe return
and we hope you will open your hearts to God's love so
that by his good grace your child will be returned. All
things are possible to them who believe.

+

I met him off the bus, little shit, little privileged berk
with his hundred-quid backpack and his tan from a
half-term ski trip and I asked him, 'Oi, plonker, did you
do that Toothwort graffiti?' and there was a brief flash
of something like confidence, something like chippiness
on his blushing face but then it was gone and he was
in tears saying sorry sorry sorry I'm so sorry and
therefore, two hours later, there we were, him and his
dad with his brother and me, scrubbing it off, silent,
none of us saying a damn thing and the thing is, what I
didn't say, obviously didn't mention, was how when my
pets died my old man always used to say 'Toothwort's
took 'em.' Perhaps that's why the whole thing freaked
me out so much and I just wanted it gone.

✝

I never properly introduced myself, I am Angela Larton, Lanny's neighbour, and I act as unofficial liaison between the authorities and the village association.

✝

I'm not genna lie to you mate it's boom time in the pub. No complaints.

✝

No secret that the police gave Noddy a warning about his prank phone calls, way back. Anyone think Noddy's a kiddie-killer?

✝

Did Lanny ever mention any other people when he was building his bower, any grown-ups he met in the woods?

✝

Yes yes, my duchess, Pete is a solid bloke, Pete has a heart of gold, Pete is salt of the earth, Pete wouldn't harm a fly, and other well-known clichés which I will regurgitate until ye my sturdy wench bringeth me my tea.

✝

Talk of the village ghoul and how to appease him. I said, Peggy you're not cheering me up much old girl.

+

I was thinking about Caroline Freeman the liaison officer, in her tight pencil skirt and patent-leather high heels, so I snuck up to the bathroom to have a wank. Self-loathing, sneaky pleasure, Caroline Freeman's skirt up round her waist, Caroline Freeman reddening, sex-blush rushing up her neck, looking over her shoulder to say don't worry, nobody can hear us and yes, yes she'd like a wet thumb in her arsehole while I fuck her, yes please, Robert, oops, good god, shame and flushed relief and guilt.

+

First I heard talking and I didn't think much of it because Alice often talks in her sleep, but I realised it was two voices, two child voices, so I woke up Gary and he heard them too, heard Alice talking to another kid, and we got up and went down the corridor and could hear, swear on my mother's life, two voices, Gary will tell you the same, and we stood outside Alice's room and listened, and they were chatting away like old friends about this and that, about their favourite foods, Alice was saying how she can't stand peanut butter and the other voice, the boy's voice said, 'Me

too, peanut butter is gross!' and Gary pushed the door
open and Alice was sitting up all alone on her bed and
we said who are you talking to, who's in the room,
Ally sweetheart, and Gary was looking in cupboards,
looking behind the door, and Alice said, 'Lanny. I was
talking to Lanny.' And I know people will judge us and
say that we're making it up, but I believe our family
has witnessed a miracle.

+

I wouldn't say this to her myself, but someone should,
that it might not harm her cause if she put some make-
up on. She looks so rough it's hard to sympathise, you
get me?

+

If he was your kid and he did come home after all this
kerfuffle how cross would you be? I'm not even joking
I'd pop a gasket.

+

She was more upset – WAIT, HEAR ME OUT – she
was more upset when Pete got beaten up than we've
seen her about Lanny, WAIT, SHUT UP, WAIT, all
I am saying, all I am saying, is that something is, OK
forget it none of you want to listen to proper ideas you
can all fuck off.

I admire what you guys do and all that, but I don't think an open-mic fundraiser is what the poor little fella would want. Not quite yet eh? He'll stay stolen if he hears the Sultans of Bling are playing.

+

What's grotesque, Theresa, is the ungodly speed of the thing, how quickly a missing child becomes a booming industry. How well-practised must we be?

+

Darkness falls at thy behest dear lord, no sin goes unpunished.

+

Dear Jolie, I don't know if you remember me but I'm Alyssa, one of the midwives who delivered Lanny. I remember him, and you, and your nice husband. I just wanted you to know that I'm thinking of you and your precious baby every day and I hope he comes home.

+

Copy gets filed, pints get poured. 'The village seems complicit in a mythologising of this unusual child, as if to accept that he is just another missing child is to do a disservice to the place, this charming village, this extra-special place.'

I phone my boss and he accuses me of being caught up in the place. Says I've gone native, gone soft. He does an impression in my accent; 'The kid was different, let's call off the search and paint some pretty pictures of him. He must have turned into an owl and flown to fucking Hogwarts to have dinner with Princess Diana.'

+

I have never seen a more guilty woman in my whole life and they need to dig the Lloyds' garden up A-sap.

Guiltier.

What?

Guiltier, not more guilty.

Do you want a smack?

+

The nice lady says, You will feel like he is calling you from the dark, like all you have is uncertainty, and there are voices, and you will remember that a child goes missing in this country every three minutes, then it will start again, You will feel like he is calling you from the dark, like all you have is uncertainty, and I look at the ceramic edge of the sink and wonder how hard I would need to throw myself at it to smash my skull open, to break open my head and rush towards the end, and remember that a child goes missing in this country every three minutes.

+

LATCHKEY LANNY: FREE TO ROAM

Parents of missing Lanny admit he was free to wander the village and they often had 'NO CLUE' where he was.

+

I stood and looked into the village and thought of Robert and Jolie in there with god knows what going on, poor Pete alone and terrified, accused of the worst possible things, and the press queued up, camped out, this hideous ecosystem of voyeurism feeding on the two of them, and these few sleepless days which feel like years, and I had a complete crisis, standing there by the stile. How can we trust anything? How can we trust other people with our children? How can we trust ourselves? How on earth have humans lived in groups? I knelt down by the stile and prayed. I felt acute despair, I felt that the missing child was the thing we most deserved, the only story left to us, lost children, and the cruelty of the thought made me retch.

I coughed and sniffed and sat there in a right godless pickle until I saw Paul Shilton coming along with his black Labrador, so I pulled myself together.

+

Specialist teams, I'm sure they are, but they have trashed the lawn and there is a broken biro in the birdbath.

+

Shook his hand actually, offered him some help with fixing his house.

+

It's been five days; it feels like months.

+

I am not 'making light of it', Marion, but let's be honest, every stiff little dick trying to be the hero of the hour, behaving as if they're action stars of a soap opera, canonising St Lanny, people who don't lift a finger for anyone else their whole miserable existence suddenly springing into Search-and-Rescue Save-the-Child-of-Light mode. Sorry if I find that a bit rich.

+

Pete?

Jolie stood gazing at me. I couldn't remember answering
the door. I didn't know what time of day it was.

Pete.

She looked drained. Grisaille. She looked semi-
transparent and spectral.

She looked as mothers presumably all over do, when
the worst thing in the world is happening to you.

I couldn't move. I stood completely locked in place like
a crumpled St Sebastian, pierced from head to toe by
her having come down here to see me.

Oh god Jolie.

She looked about my broken home, at the graffiti and
ruined things, at the police tape and duplicate copies of
official papers, at the paint thrown across my sink and
sideboard.

She looked at the sprayed magenta word PEADO on
my kitchen wall.

She walked to me and laid her forehead on my shoulder.

I didn't hold her I just stood.

She said Sorry and I rested my cheek on her head and
said No.

No.

She said Sorry.

Sorry.

She said I know you would never

I shook my head and held her.

+

Propped on the bar, Mick is telling me, Don't be so
naïve, sweetheart, missing kids, murdered girls, raped
and hunted women, trafficked youngsters, killer
parents, sex dungeons, bodies in bags and under patios,
it's a billion-dollar industry actively encouraged by
the powers that be oop – he bends to pick a dropped
peanut up off the patterned carpet and rises reddened
from the exertion.

Always, oop – he belches in his cupped hand – Always
follow the money. He is telling me about tabloid
economics and who sits at the tables of power. The
hairs in his nostrils, coated with amber tar, waggle as
he talks, as he gazes constantly at my tits, as he unlocks
the mysteries of the world and I wonder what to cook
for my tea.

+

Readers of this column will know that I like to take a situation at face value. So let's look at her face. This woman, this model of English pain, with her nice bone structure, natural hair and kissable lips, this woman is clearly living every mother's worst nightmare. Oh yes, she's quite the tragic queen of England; our Terrified EveryMum specially selected from all the mums in similar situations because her face and her village are so picturesque. So far so familiar. But what if something is hiding in plain sight? Isn't it, dear reader, our job to peek behind the performance? I'm not alone in this country wondering what it is about Mrs Lloyd's performance that doesn't sit right with me. What is it about this professional actress, trained to manipulate and convince audiences, that isn't quite convincing me? What is it about this writer of an (according to the would-be publisher) 'immaculately plotted psychological thriller' (if you've read the leaked pages you know it's a *vicious* book) that doesn't seem quite able to convince as the star of this family drama? To be clear, I don't think she's a murderer, and we'll see what comes to light in the weeks and months, maybe years to come, but let me say now, dear readers, there's something about Jolie Lloyd that rings alarm bells with me.

✝

Out of control now, this miracle stuff. A four-year-old boy who can hardly hold a pencil has written a letter from Lanny, saying he's fine, but he's with the angels. Handwriting and vocabulary categorically beyond the reach of any four-year-old and his nursery teacher was there the whole time, watching it happen. The TV cameras have descended and the family are turning down six-figure sums, the whole thing's deeply worrying if you ask me.

+

I spoke to him all the time. I knew him really really well. And my mum once went in their house for a coffee.

+

If you want to know about miracles ask Peggy, I said, knowing full well Peggy hasn't said a single word to any journalist and nor would she.

+

You'll never guess what I've just seen. I have just seen Robert standing in the pub car park with Pete and they were hugging each other. I don't mean like a quick crisis hug, I'm talking they were squeezing the life out of each other. Pete with his black eye for god's sake it's just heartbreaking. Both of them shaking and clinging to each other. I've got a heart of stone as you know but I was very moved by the sight.

+

We are but pitiful narrative creatures, Mrs Brailsford, obsessing over the agony of not knowing. Sisyphus, Atlas, Echo, all those poor souls, now us. It is the oldest story of them all; never-ending pain.

+

I'm not listening to a single word of what this well-meaning psychologist or officer or doctor or liaison person or whatever she is is saying to me, but my parents are listening, and Robert's usually good at listening, Robert's all smart and smelling nice after his shower, my hands are so dry they've cracked open across the knuckles, what a good listener, writing stuff down and then, what?

What did you say?

You.

What did you say?

She said, We've recovered a packet of Lanny's letters, they were handed in this morning, they were in the bracken bushes along the side of the common by Ghost Pilot Lane and at present they're being looked at by . . .

+

And that's when Jolie went completely fucking mad.

+

And that's when I went completely fucking mad.

I caused a decent scene. I just could not sit there
listening to that woman tell me that we had to
seriously consider that Lanny had done something
to himself, that Lanny was 'evidently' based on this
latest 'evidence' up to some unusual stuff and the
psychological profiler would like to come back and ask
some more questions about Lanny and his behaviour
and conversations you might have had with him, and
yes, the dam broke and I had a violent rage the like of
which I never imagined I was capable of, and I would
like to not apologise, not one bit, no regrets. I would
have liked to keep smashing and screaming. I told
that woman that if she didn't phone her superiors and
bring me those letters within the hour then I would
gouge the pretty blue eyes out of her head and eat
them.

+

I was thinking they were beginning to understand
Lanny, his ability to wriggle and twist free from every
attempt to grasp him. I was used to this. I've been

asking myself Where is Lanny for years. What is up with that boy?

+

A team of six of us, back out looking. Combing the woods.

Pete joined us later, calling up at the orchard and back around to Howarth's fence. You never know. Can't just hope and wait.

+

It's hard to describe the disruption, the damage it does to normal thought processes. It's hard to convey the sheer trauma of it, everything warped, inarticulate longing, unquenchable thirst for information, smashed right up against mundane orders from the brain or belly. A most tiresome dialogue all the time; look at me drinking a cup of tea while my grandson is still out there, look at me folding my daughter's clothes as if that will bring back the missing child. Lanny Lanny Lanny all of us, the drone of his name buzzing in every possible bit of mental space. The closest experience to it I can think of is when I hid under a desk in 1963 with my classmates waiting for a nuclear bomb to drop on us. It was coming. It is coming.

+

Half a dozen bits of paper, tied with green garden
string, wrapped in clingfilm. Everyone whispering,
That's them. That's the notes. Lanny hid notes in the
bushes.

+

No adequate response that I know of to such a thing.

+

Now beneath us is growing, up above us is growing.
Make a sword!
Collect rainwater.
Mix it with human spit and a pinch of earth
And the mixture will be magic, only for you,
The green man mixes his potions
And stitches me an autumn coat for my journey
Lick sap. Pack a bag.
Get ready and wait
The mixture will sing your plan.

+

She sits in the garden all afternoon reading them over
and over.

I overhear one of them saying, Won't forget today in a
hurry.

People come and go.

All these experts and journalists and kind strangers
all shivering and flinching from the loudly abnormal
nature of this.

Ideas in his head.

Look at them now.

I overhear one of them saying, Bizarre doesn't cover it
mate.

The tone of speculation has shifted completely. There's
hitherto been a child-catcher in all our minds, a stealer,
a man harming Lanny. He's grown every day, grown
fangs and sadistic skills, grown miraculous law-evading
powers and travel agent expertise. The letters seem to
have banished that man.

I overhear one of them say on his phone, Encourage
the volunteers to think like a child, like a very strange
child.

  ✝

Old man's beard and ivy and moss, pass through
hundreds of seasons unharmed.
The world isn't ruined if you're planted in it. Trees are
in charge.
Rain finds a way around me, runs off me,

I'm waxed leaves and hard flint, storing tomorrow's
sunshine in my bark, invisible.

+

I go and sit out there with her and we read the letters
together and we don't say anything.

+

None of us said a thing, just watched them. Just utterly
bizarre. Rick was stood there with the Achieving Best
Evidence Guidelines in a plastic folder like a total
lemon muttering 'what the actual fuck' again and
again.

+

I was thinking: what a shapeless life. I miss my
commute. I miss going back and forth. I turn an idea
over in my mind, secretly, gazing at Lanny's strange
words, *Rain finds a way around me*. The idea, chucked
between the hands of my mind like a hot baked roll,
is that I don't miss him, that I don't have any feelings
about him. If I wasn't central in the drama of his being
missing, would I actually care that he's gone. Is this
taboo? Is this some scandalous truth about me? It's
awful, this secret. It's possibly the only clear thinking
I have ever done, out here, alone with my bereft
wife, reading these weird spells or plans or whatever

they are that Lanny's left us. Yes, I tell myself, this
is the truth. I am thinking clearly. I am privileged to
know this now, about us all. None of us actually feel
anything for anyone else. It's all pretend.

✝

Those morbid folk seem to have cleared off, probably
moved on to a fresher tragedy somewhere. Tribulation
chasers.

✝

Carla, please, we are dying of thirst here. Missing
child or no missing child, we shouldn't have to wait six
minutes for two pints of Foster's.

✝

OK, monsieur moral high ground, let's suppose you
had Jolie's manuscript, would the value of that book
not increase with every column inch about young
Lanny? Is she not the most bankable unpublished
author in the country today save for a royal?

✝

Property prices in the greenbelt, my friend. Immune to
troubles. Recessions come and go, children are born, go
missing, grow up and die. It is our job to build. Here's
to our green and pleasant land, for what it's worth.

+

The very idea of a safe place is tyrannical.

+

We all feel foolish.

+

Gravitas and rebellious gaiety, I pray.

+

Faith in signs.

+

If you're not scared, you're not doing it right.

+

Charmless times.

+

Still looking.

+

Peggy's back at her antique gate. Rubbing the worn wood. Holding on.

Listening for endings.

Waiting.

3

I was caught up in the duvet, Jolie wasn't with me, and whatever stone platform this part of the world was built on had rolled in its bed and we were on the tilt, and hidden things were poking through, breaking the surface. I looked out of the window and saw the prow of a huge chalk ship edging into the garden, hundreds of feet high, glowing in the moon.

I was caught up in the sheets, Robert wasn't with me, maybe I was on the sofa, and the house had been turned inside out, gravel on the floor, ivy on the walls, a thick wedge of pine needles lodged in my throat, choking me. I looked down at my body and saw that it was glistening wet and dappled like a slug; convulsing, shining and sticky.

I was caught up in my clothes, asleep at the kitchen table, soft and forgiving sleep, and I had been enjoying my dreams and the table was warm and I realised it was made of living human skin, clean-smelling, podgy-pulsing alive, whispering wake up Pete, soft expanse hot against my cheek, young and alive against my old face, wake up Pete.

Peter Blythe looks down in the ripe dead-of-night and sees that on his kitchen table, right where he's been sleeping, is a small card. It's an invitation. He reads it and the shock of it makes his flesh tighten and his tired heart beat faster. Pete doesn't hesitate, he splashes his face with cold water at the kitchen tap, he hurries into the bathroom and pisses, and then he pulls on his coat and boots. He is muttering to himself and doesn't even take a key or turn off his lights or close his front door, he hurries out of his house, hurries to where he's been invited to go.

It is moonbright, hardly dark but very much middle of the night, and there is a dead-ish smell of duck or goose shit, some waterbird's droppings, mixed with diesel or grease. Strange evening, thinks Pete, as he hurries up the road to the high street. How odd. Pete stops. He's coming to the village street as if from the other side, as if returning home. As if he's walking in the mirror image or reverse impression of the village. I get you, thinks Pete, the village is a woodcut print, and I'm walking here in the cut block itself. No matter, he's half asleep. It's cold. Just some trick of the night. Pete blows his breath out neat and funnelled, cut through pursed lips like a smoker or a flautist. He stamps up the street as if a strong excitable dog is leading him. He's confused, again, because it's all reversed, because he's coming down towards Peggy, rather than up towards her, leaning on her gate, but he hasn't passed the hall. She should be on the other side. Someone has turned this bloody village inside out, Pete thinks to himself, but he doesn't mind, he's too busy to mind. Peggy looks young and beautiful and her gate is not yet worn with most-of-a-century's rubbing, and her soldier brothers are knocking a ball about in the moonlight behind her. Pete walks over to greet her. 'Go,' she says. '*Go*, Peter, no time to stop, you've got to get there, he won't want you to be late.'

So he smiles and waves and hurries onwards, up what should be down the hill, to the village hall.

The lights are on but he's nervous, suddenly, and wishes he knew the time, wishes he knew what to expect. He's never involved in the village shows. What time of year is it? What could it be?

There are hurried footsteps and Pete flinches, as men recently beaten are wont to flinch, but it's only Jolie. God, he's pleased to see Jolie.

She holds, crumpled in her grasp, an invitation.

More steps, and towards them through the clean platinotype sharpness of the night comes Robert.

'Robert?' says Jolie.

'Pete?' says Robert.

They all hold out their small pieces of cardboard.

DEAD PAPA TOOTHWORT PRESENTS
LANNY: THE ENDING
VILLAGE HALL
TONIGHT

They go in, clustered and shuffling like three nervous children. The heavy wooden door clunks shut behind them.

Slicing through the village hall's usual smell (dried modelling clay, pensioner dust, flower arranging foam, urine, smelly plimsolls) is a powerful stench which each of the three invited guests can't quite place. It's almost the oddly pleasing smell of molten asphalt, but it's natural, ripe, green-on-the-turn, sweet, with something dead or decaying within it. All three guests wobble there in the entrance, as if drugged, measuring memories against the smell, acclimatising themselves.

They have plastic cups of red wine in their hands, and little pink raffle tickets. The hall lights are harsh strip-lights, buzzing.

The three guests find themselves seated. Nobody has said a word.

'Welcome,' says a voice from the stage. 'Well, here we all are. So: Ticket number 1? Pink number 1 anyone?'

On the small stage is a six-foot-high drawing of a man. He is Lanny's shoulderless man, from the very first art lesson with Pete. He is swaying slightly, with empty legs and sloppy oblongs for feet. He has a box-like chest. He has no neck, and atop his smiling face are a dozen neat strands of hair standing anti-gravity tall and spiked. Out of the middle of his body, at nipple height, shoot two long arms ending in circles with podgy fingers barely attached. He waggles his stiff horizontal arms.

'You'd recognise me anywhere, right, Pete?' he says.

He speaks in Pete's voice.

Jolie and Robert turn to look at Pete, who is seated in the middle, and there are tears making glistening progress down Pete's old cheeks, but he says nothing.

The man beckons at Pete clumsily with his rigid and flat badly drawn hands.

'Pink ticket 1? Come here, Pete. You've got the first ticket. Peter?'

Pete does not move, cannot move.

The smiling face is fixed and says again, in Pete's own voice, 'Come now old man.'

Slowly, as if the chair legs are attached to invisible winches in the drawn man's eyes, Pete's seat is dragged towards the stage. Pete is sobbing, soundlessly. His feet slide across the floor, caught backwards under his chair like the feet of a dead man. Hopeless. His hands lie pathetically crossed in his lap. He is shaking his head.

He is hauled steadily to the platform upon which the drawn man stands. The chair bumps against the stage blocks.

Pete peers up.

'Fix me,' says the drawing.

Pete shakes his head.

The smiling face of the child's drawing speaks again, as if playing a recording, and Pete hears himself speaking to Lanny, that first afternoon.

'Right, Lanny. Where do your arms come out? You've got this bloke's arms coming out the side of his body, what do you reckon?'

Pete shakes his head.

The drawing shouts:

'FIX ME!'

Robert and Jolie suddenly crack into shrieking yelps of encouragement; 'Fix him!' 'Fix him!'

Pete gets up and climbs to the stage, his knees cracking with effort, sniffing and wiping his nose on his sleeve.

'Fix him!'

He grabs one of the drawn man's arms and wrenches it off. He drops it and yanks off the other arm.

The drawing sways and grins and sticks his tongue out, but it's not a tongue, it's a thick builder's pencil. He spits it onto the stage and Pete bends to pick it up.

'Fix me, Mad Pete.'

Pete looks back at Jolie and Robert but they've become shiny-faced dummies, plastic sports fans, grinning and jiggling in their seats.

He raises the pencil and draws a line. It holds. He works away around the box of the man's chest, good clean lines, and sure enough the marks appear, are real, are joined to each other and suspended, are growing, drafted growth from the shoulders of the man, one arm, two arms, well-drawn arms, and the drawing bends and flexes his new limbs as they appear. From the flat crudity of Lanny's drawing rises something modelled, accomplished and true to muscled animated life. Pete works fast.

'Go, Pete!' says plastic Robert.

'Go, Pete!' Clap clap clap, Jolie smacks her thighs robotically. 'Go, Pete!' Clap clap clap.

The drawing speaks again, as Pete once spoke:

'Now the head, Lanny. Might I ask you to consider your own self and see if there's anything between your head and your chest?'

Pete reaches and tugs the head up, decapitating the drawing momentarily, holds the face aloft with one arm while he sketches in a good thick neck, the bump of an Adam's apple, the slight suggestion of sinews, and he drops it back on and shades the chin and neck together.

'Thank you!' booms the hybrid giant – half child's doodle, half accomplished life-study – throbbing and more-than-three-dimensional, 'oh yes!' and he reaches down and closes his arms around Pete, embracing him, and Pete cries, shaking, with his arms by his sides, clutching his pencil. The man squeezes him with strong new arms, proper arms, and he presses his powerful chin down, and Pete is wheezing and struggling for breath, trapped in the embrace. He is constricted and powerless and the drawn man starts to sing the song that Lanny sang that day, and the shrill imposter Robert and not-real-Jolie's voices join in unison, from behind, and Pete can't breathe, he can only listen, and it sounds horrendous in the adults' voices, a child's absent-minded song turned into a feverish chant, turned into something threatening, and he starts to feel sleepy, he is being squeezed so hard, he feels like a child in the grip of a circling fever, and he starts to slip off, he starts to slide into the warm place beyond this brutal hug, towards the comfort he feels is there inside the song somewhere, inside Lanny's song.

'Limmon aah, bitter car, lemmen arr, fennem arr, mennem are, witter kah, fitterkarr,' they sing. The living drawing squeezes him and Pete is limp now, hanging in the hug, diminished, like an empty costume of an old man. Jolie and Robert are loudly, brashly singing, 'Limmon aah, bitter car, lemmen arr,' stamping their feet, clapping their hands, and the drawn man leans down and whispers in Pete's ear, in Pete's voice, 'You can see him, can't you? As a teenager? You hope, don't you, Pete. You HOPE! You can see Lanny, a bit embarrassed to see you, maybe with his mates at the bus stop, a bit of stubble, a broken voice, and he doesn't say hello, but he nods, and there's a conspiratorial glance, a bond of sorts, yes? *All right Pete.* Can you see teenage Lanny, Pete? Is this one of your endings?'

Pete is fading, slipping into darkness, the hall is a memory, the dark is wrapping him up, and he smiles at the suggestion, because yes, that's exactly what he's seen, what he's yearned for, and so he answers,

'Yes.'

And they are plunged into darkness, all three guests back on their seats, terrified. Silent, frozen and mute.

There is a rustling, squelching, a snapping sound of footsteps on plants, of stalks being squashed.

'Let there be light,' says Toothwort, in the voice of a young English woman. She chuckles, a bubbling flirtatious laugh. 'A good start, tip-top work from old Mad Pete!'

The lights come on and Robert sees that she is perfect. Painful for a faithful bloke to behold.

'Now, pink ticket 2? Robert, are you ready to play?'

Toothwort beckons with a floral finger.

Robert leaps up from his chair. He is wearing expensive Lycra jogging gear. Jolie and Pete are gone. It is just Robert and Toothwort.

'Ready as I'll ever be,' he says.

Toothwort teeters over in six-inch hollyhock heels, unsteady on the spongy floor of parasitic plants. She almost slips but Robert catches her by the elbow. Her smell is dizzying.

'Thanks,' she squeezes his hand damply. 'Now concentrate, babe,' she whispers, breathing wet musk onto his neck, 'time for your first test.'

There is a mobile phone floating at head height in a pool of its own blue-screen luminescence.

Robert stretches his calf muscles and steps forwards. His elbow grazes her breast as he passes and his penis throbs slightly in his tight sports leggings.

'Ready!'

He plucks the mobile phone from mid-air before him. He knows his way around a device like this.

'Now, Robert Lloyd,' says sexy Toothwort. 'Look at these images. Is this one of your endings?'

He gazes at the screen, brow furrowed, occasionally flicking it with his finger. He is not pleased with what he sees.

Toothwort is quietly panting, hissing, releasing grassy aromas.

'Robert? Is this one of your endings?'

He shakes his head and turns the phone away. 'No, oh no.'

He straightens and turns to Toothwort, 'Please, no . . .'

'Say what you see, Robert,' says Toothwort, whose smooth flesh has started sprouting small shoots and petals. Her pretty teeth are softening into bruised white berries; her lips are mottled runner beans.

Robert is sweating, he has dark patches under his arms and on his chest. He unzips his Lycra top and wipes his brow.

'Oh god no. Please.'

'Yes, Robert?'

'It's, it's Lanny. He's being . . . I don't want to say.'

'You have to say what you see, Robert. Otherwise we can't move forward.'

'He's . . . He's being abused. Being hurt.'

'And is this one of your endings? Have you seen this?'

Robert gazes at the mobile phone. He scratches his head like a schoolboy faced with tricky arithmetic.

'I'm sorry to rush you, Robert, but I have to ask, is this

one of your endings? Is this something you saw for your son?'

Robert turns away from the phone, eyes glistening, stares at the space where Jolie and Pete were, and says, 'Yes.'

The phone is gone.

'Bravo, Robert,' says Toothwort, who is now completely covered in rotting flowers, a damp edgeless plant-nymph, her polished TV-ready accent crumbling into a gravelly drawl, her eyes and mouth leaking oily green fluid.

'That was very brave. Of course you've seen those images. Very brave to admit that. Now, screen two please.'

A new phone has appeared and Robert strides over and begins scrolling determinedly, braced for more pain, but as he gazes into the glowing air he smiles. He unclenches his spare fist and chuckles.

He turns to smile at Toothwort behind him.

'What is it, Robert? Is it one of your endings?'

'It's wonderful! It's Lanny, handsome as anything. Alive! In his late twenties, early thirties? In a really well-cut suit, grinning like anything, with a beautiful girl on his arm. His green eyes blazing! Really lovely suit. Lanny alive and well and getting married!'

'That's adorable, Robert. Is this one of your endings?'

And Robert is so relieved, so lightened and unburdened, so carried away, enchanted by those images of his son that he replies, without thinking, 'Yes!'

The hall is plunged into darkness.

No more sportswear, no more phones. Robert is shivering, cold sweat on his temples and on the back of his neck. He can't speak, or move, or remember what he's done wrong.

'Oh dear, Robert. Failure. You must tell the truth at times like this. Pete managed it, didn't he?'

Toothwort wraps him up in a gaseous embrace, slides him across the hall and dumps him, limp and dreaming, into a plastic chair.

'Not good at all, Robert.'

Robert.

Robert?

'Robert?' Jolie is tapping him on the shoulder but he's fast asleep.

'Pete?'

The two men are sprawled on their chairs, snoring.

She looks around the hall and it is just the hall. She seems to be back in real life, or she has woken up, or she is alive, or no longer having a nightmare. She wonders whether she should go back, she wonders if the police officers who are outside twenty-four hours a day noticed her leaving, or perhaps they've gone, perhaps they've all given up, perhaps it's all over or was never happening. She rubs her face with her dry palms and breathes in the cold stale air of the hall, all the christenings and eighteenths and retirements and jubilees and anniversaries; the wakes, the parent and toddler mornings. She breathes in the flesh particles of generations of villagers before her and it tastes like mould and wet tweed.

'Ah, finally,' says a voice from the dark corner of the hall, 'just the two of us. Pink ticket number 3. The important one. The decider.'

He is sitting, cross-legged, in the most beautiful creation she has ever seen; a sculpture, a shrine, a twinkling altar made of natural things. She walks towards it across the crinkly leaves, twigs and mossy floor of the hall.

It's Lanny's bower. Dead Papa Toothwort is sitting waiting for her inside. He's dressed as a garden centre ornament, a mass-produced green man for the shed door, bushy oak-leaf eyebrows, podgy cheeks, ivy hair and wheatsheaf beard. She can see cast marks on his cheeks, and the sticky remnants of a yellow price tag. He shrugs and winks.

The bower rises from the floor like a cupped hand, the bulk of it made from twigs woven and packed, expertly threaded, held together with stems and tendrils, bracken and mud, honeysuckle vines patiently stripped and woven, densely insulated with moss and mulch squeezed in the gaps, bedded down and set through a season or two. The bower is strong and alluring.

'And look at the detail,' says Toothwort, and she sees, as she stoops and peers inside, that birds' eggs, pebbles and conkers, snail shells and bones decorate the interior, like a grotto, like a tiny little pagan church lovingly decorated. Layers like a geological cross-section rise from the base; a ring of knotted straw, of lichen-clad bark, of broken crockery combed from the beechwood's hidden dumping grounds. Everything stitched together for the good of the overall design, for the depth of the welcome. It's awe-inspiring. She sits next to Toothwort, and she trusts him.

He tilts his head, questioning.

She nods.

He looks in her eyes as if for permission.

She holds her breath.

'Please,' she says.

And so Dead Papa Toothwort gently breaks open time, and shows her Lanny.

The bower disappears, all is unbuilt, and they are sitting on the floor of the woods in dappled morning sunlight. In comes the sound of her child, singing, Lanny's strange half-song half-hum chit-chat, and he is among them, in his school shorts and a T-shirt, pottering, planning, darting about, delicate and focused, laying a few early markers, clearing the ground, drawing the perimeter with a stick, off again, back with a bundle, off again, like a time-lapse nature video, she sees him a thousand times a second, her little winged thing, attending to his creation, flickering sun-up sun-down, days layered upon patient days, and she realises their life at home, his time at school, what she thought of as his real existence, was only a place he visited.

It is so good to see him. Bliss. He is not real, he is just the memory of Lanny on the things that he touched; she knows that. He is transparent, in and out of actuality like the light itself, but still, his mannerisms, his voice, his gorgeous body language, his extraordinary green eyes. She watches and sees the bower become part of the wood. A deer pokes its head in the entrance, then a middle-aged lady with an OS map, then a squirrel, then Lanny is lying on the floor singing at the top of his voice, grabbing armfuls of mulch and grinning, then he is sobbing, punching the floor, then he is hunched over writing his strange little recipes, his letters, his plans, then he is gone and the bower is half built, waiting, and warmth brings odd dusty knives of light into the space. It's a sacred place. Toothwort's concrete skin has softened and rustled into life, he's made of real leaves now, and he smiles at Jolie and mouths the word 'Watch'.

The walls come up around them, Lanny packing and fiddling, tweaking, knotting and tutting, whistling and chatting, and Jolie feels his breath on her cheek. She closes her eyes and feels the twitching pulse of days and nights, and when she opens them the walls are built and Lanny is darting in and out between her and Toothwort, adding snail shells and chalk, fitting nuts and hard berries, dead insects and interesting twigs into every possible gap, and then she sees other kids she recognises briefly darting into the bower, laughing, and one of them smashes a wall, and Lanny is back patiently fixing, smiling as he works and then he is lying down and he looks his mother straight in the eyes. She smiles and her child smiles back.

He sings *'Say Your Prayers and Be Good Too, Or Dead Papa Toothwort Is Coming for You'* and he closes his eyes.

He says, *'Old man's beard and ivy and moss, pass through hundreds of seasons unharmed.'*

'Lanny? Love?'

He can't hear her.

Crouched across from her, Toothwort has darkened, his foliate head has ripened into mould, fungus and brown ripples, sweaty, heavy with rot and enzymes. He smells like natural truth, like sex and death. It's comforting, and Jolie hugs herself and inhales. The room is juddering, snoring, humming. Toothwort seems to be shrinking, shrivelling in on himself, the mushrooms darkening and turning to wet clumps, turning to soggy knobbly autumn compost.

He gazes at her. He lifts one hand, which changes from a perfect blusher mushroom into a ball of flies and is gone. He raises the faint outline of his other hand to his lips and blows her a kiss.

He says something but all she hears is a wheeze. He is sinking into the ground.

'What?' she says. 'What?'

He seems to whisper 'follow' or 'for you' and his face darkens like a stain as he dissolves.

She sees that Lanny is packing things into his bag, preparing to leave. Night is creeping in through the gaps of the walls.

'No!'

Jolie panics, she tries to reach over to her son but she is locked in place. Her legs are fixed. She can't move.

Lanny hops up, grabs his bag and ducks out of the bower.

'Wait!'

He is running away, up the track, past the Elvis Hair Hawthorn, over the stile and into the dark wood, darting through the trees, leaping over stumps and brambles, his rucksack bouncing on his back.

'Lanny!'

She tries to give chase, but she is only watching. She is only vision, no body. She follows but not at her own speed, not touching the ground or feeling the weather.

She is caught between what's real and what's not, moving through the partial air, through the solid trees. She is like a camera panning across a set. It is sheer torment but she is also suffused by a deep gratitude, the drug-like bliss of appreciation for what she is being shown. She is being shown Lanny. They are up in Hatchett Wood.

As the steep flank of the old wood meets the fenced rim of the managed fields there's a sparser hundred yards of thinner, younger trees. It feels like a frontier, a meeting place between she's not sure what. It's poised, this place, ready and waiting like an empty stage.

She reaches Lanny as he is kneeling, scrabbling, pulling aside a man-made blanket of branches. He uncovers the big metal lid of a drain. He uses a screwdriver to pop open the cover, then he gets his fingers under and heaves it up and over. It lands with a heavy whump on the leafy carpet.

Jolie calls out but she knows he can't hear.

Lanny's camp is a disused storm drain, dug into the hill, invisible unless you walked right to it. It's a perfect boy-sized space, a den cut into the floor of the forest. A brilliant place to hide.

She sees him climb in.

'Lanny, no!'

She watches him sit on the metal grille, three feet beneath the surface, and she watches him unpack his notes, his pens, his knotted charms, his book, his little bottle of water and his snack bar.

She watches in horror as he fidgets on the grating beneath him. Shuffling. She sees him recognise the click and shift, sees the awful split-second in which he realises something's wrong. A look of worry crosses his face as a black bruise of cloud-shadow thumps across the clearing.

There's a pop and a screech.

The little metal hinges snap, the rusted grate comes away from the derelict walls of the drain and drops. The world gives way. The child and all his things plummet into blackness.

Lanny wails in pain from the floor of the dark pit and Jolie roars and scratches at the air but she isn't there. She is helpless and silent. He cannot climb out and she cannot climb in.

Out of the hole she hears screaming and crying, shouting for help, a voice growing hoarse with wailing. The sounds of her child's mind serrated by fear. Embarrassment and shame and yelps of baffled hurt.

Pleading ow ow ows and sudden screeches. He begs to be found. He tries every possible scaling or scrabbling or searching for hand-holds. He is stuck. He tries many things. He throws his book out and it lands, sadly, open midway through. Lanny screams and bellows for his parents. For his mates. For his teachers. For his friend Pete. He calls for them all.

The moon spreads a flattening blanket of light across the woods. She cannot bear it. She desperately wants to peer into the hole. To reach him. She yearns to climb in with him. But she knows she is watching a replay, she is peering from a fold in time. Time. *Perfect time of night*, in the woods, watching your son disappear.

She thinks of the painted Virgin, a fantasy mother, with a gap on her lap where the future should be. Hands curled round an absence, caressing the empty space where her son once was.

Time accelerates and pauses, wobbles and misbehaves in a way that is familiar to Jolie, speeding through the dark hours so that she doesn't have to listen to the sobs of her son and then holding still while he's quiet, and the terrible closeness between them is all there is. There is some kind of grace in the unreal encounter, as when he was very new, when he was a tiny baby first breathing and feeding.

He rations his water, but takes the final tiny sip in the morning of the second day.

There are great stretches of silence. There are glimpses of the week she has lived. A policeman traipses along the pinched top lip of the wood taking photos and Jolie screams, hopelessly. She shouts – voicelessly – that he is *here*, he is just here. How is it possible that he hasn't been found?

A team of volunteers with neon yellow jackets walk the edge of the field whacking at the long grass with walking sticks.

A badger trundles over and noses the open paperback disinterestedly.

A man comes close to the hole. He is smoking a cigarette and calling Lanny's name, kicking up leaves as he goes. He is not searching as if expecting to find. Lanny must be sleeping and does not call out. The man wanders off and another night begins.

In time she hears song, curling up out of the hole as Lanny starts to sing. A garland of part-rhymes and nursery lines, bastardised pop tunes and repetitive sobbed or chanted pleas to be rescued. His hope begins to fade.

He talks of his terrible thirst, of being freezing cold, of his own shit and piss and tears. Jolie's heart is broken. She hears him saying his weird prayers and he shakes them empty and spits them out. *Now beneath us is growing, up above us is growing.*

Collect rainwater, he yells, disgusted, pleading, dreaming of water. He licks the mossy walls of his cell. He sucks the dirty clumps of moss beneath him. He hates himself. He knows enough about human bodies to know that his will fail if he can't drink water.

On the fourth or fifth evening Lanny speaks directly to his mum. He says sorry. He tells her he loves her. He whispers stories of gratitude and regret. He says he is so thirsty he could invent the idea of water every second. He says sorry sorry sorry sorry sorry. Sorry, Mum. Sorry, Dad. Tell Arch and Alf and Mrs Lucas sorry tell Pete sorry tell Gran sorry. He describes his bower and hopes she finds it. He sings of the terrible strangeness of being alive and the agony of being trapped in a cold damp drain when his bed is half a mile from here. He sobs and asks to be found.

'Please find me.'

He says, 'Mum, I'm dying. I'm dying, Mum.'

Much later, eyes closed, curled on his side, shivering, he remembers. Just as he is sliding towards dark sleep, just as his tongue is hardening and his blood is slowing, exhausted, he whispers, 'Toothwort?'

Jolie's flesh prickles and the whole scene sharpens and snaps alive. The air is crisp. The forest is awake.

Lanny says, 'Toothwort? You promised. I'm thirsty. Please?'

'Toothwort?'

Fifty yards from Lanny's trap a beech sapling shivers and thickens itself loosely into the shape of a little human being.

Jolie watches him and smiles as she realises.

Of course.

He is a child.

She supposes he must be wearing something like his original skin. Verdant. He stands calm and small against the undergrowth, a green-stem changeling. He is naked in the dusk, glowing. Flickering thin edges of leaf or stalk take the weight of his steps, become mammal, then melt back into plant. He seems happy, now. The edgeless peace that hangs in the air at this time of evening seems to emanate from him, immemorial. Jolie watches him inch forwards, radiant, and she realises he is good. A god, perhaps.

He tiptoes towards his friend, trapped in the forest floor. He reaches the hole and lies down, peering over the lid.

He speaks to the boy.

Lanny Greentree, you remind me of me.

He stands. He seems to be looking at Jolie. She can't hold the sight of him steady. Her brain and her eyes don't know what messages to send each other, so there is no resolution. He blinks and glimmers in and out of solid form, camouflaged or non-existent against the woodland, against her disbelief. But she's like the well-trained dreamer who interrupts or haunts their own dreams with knowledge of the waking pain to come, so she concentrates. She watches so hard she might break.

Toothwort holds one arm over the hole and grows what he needs.

An apple takes flesh from the open cup of his palm, rising slowly from a splodge of green matter, russeting as it rounds. A freckly, perfectly realised apple, just right for the job. He drops it in to Lanny. Then he is gone, then back again more hesitant, then circling the hole, less a figure than a rippling energy between things. Then he is standing very still, concentrating, rocking on the breeze, and he wriggles his fingers and there are hazelnuts. He shakes and claps and there is a plum. Then a handful of cherries. Some beech masts and wild garlic, dozens of little wild strawberries, raspberries and loganberries, ripening and dropping off him, into the hole to keep the child alive.

The miracle harvest of his best intentions seems to please him, as if he's been waiting a long time to save this life. He throws in blackberries and bilberries, pacing in a circle around the hiding place. He listens to the startled noises of feasting below. Toothwort laughs and it's the sound of a hundred small birds taking flight. He hunches and makes a cup of his two hands, stomata closed, a good leafy vessel, and fills it with water, cold spring water from the chalk aquifers beneath. He pours it down for the child to drink.

Every living thing is involved.

Night falls, and Dead Papa Toothwort is done.

Jolie wakes. She's been lying on the forest floor. How long she has been there, she can't tell. It's moon-peep and chilly and she's lost her bearings.

There's a small voice in the trembling wood. Calling her.

It's hard to see, but there's a faint glow from the tree line above her and she knows she's not alone. She knows she's close so she shouts, 'I'm here!'

There's a thick barrier of ivy and bramble, fallen trees, wire and rotten posts, and she knows she's close, pushing through, kicking through bracken clumps, but she's making no progress, the tree line is the same distance, it's all thicket and tangles and she remembers it being more open, lighter, closer, she can't make progress, she's on her knees again, and she can't see, struggling against the slope, feeling as if she might fall backwards off the earth and then 'Go!' she is shoved from behind, two firm hands, strength of another body, support of some kind. Yelling as if in battle, Robert is there with her. They scramble up nearer to the spot and it's familiar but not as she saw it, there are logs and bits of old car and huge flints trip her and the bramble is thick between her and the clearing. Jolie rips at the tangled briar and her hands are bleeding and Robert kicks again and again at the fortress of weeds and thorns and two more strong hands push on Jolie's back as she almost topples backwards and Pete is there with them, 'Go!' Pete is pulling at the undergrowth, stamping nettles down, rolling great lumps of mouldy wood away, roaring, 'I've got you,' and the three of them push forwards as if guided. A trinity of desperate effort. They rip and tug and flail and Jolie calls for Lanny.

She screams his name. Pete and Robert join in, shouting for him. They push and shove his name into the undergrowth, into pockets of darkness, finding suggestions of paths, and then they break into open space, familiar smells and wet leaves, a pile of broken hundred-year-old glass bottles, a traffic cone, knowable rubbish, contemporary litter, a plastic sports bottle Robert recognises, he shrieks and the other two join him and Jolie is saying that this is the spot, this is the place. There's a zip-loc bag, cleanish and recent, a paperback kid's book, they are finding things, they are yelling with each discovery, and there are dogs with them now, hectic, pushing and panting, sniffing and barking, it's dark but flickering and there are other people, many voices, with torches, with gloves and tough boots, with clarity of purpose, huge shears, vehicles, the undergrowth is de-tangled by lights, the ground is suddenly just ground, small flat intimate place, step aside please, stand clear, there is a metal lid, then there is a concrete square, an open hole, radio crackle and distant blue lights, yells and discord and sirens and messages, screens, bellowing people calling for space, calling for equipment, for proper crime-scene care, calling for calm, and Jolie screaming for quiet, lying down, reaching in. The little patch of light around the strange drain, hand signals, bleeps, panting and swearing, and all of a sudden in the forest, it stops.

Everyone quiet.

Just a mother and the name of her child.

PEGGY

False things, endings. Sustenance for fools and never what they claim to be.

Nevertheless.

I died the summer after they pulled Lanny out of the drain in Hatchett Wood. My heart stopped, but my body stood holding the gate for a further fifteen minutes. Several people said good afternoon to my cooling corpse. Eventually a light wind toppled me over. I lay on the path for an hour or two until I realised I was free to go, could just up and leave the old carrion Peggy lying on the path.

I go up to Lanny's spot most nights and it is markedly transformed, that place. Close to the spot where the earth was disturbed a boyish sapling stands. It never grows. It's lad height, healthy, and catches the evening sun.

There is a gentler breath up there, a different depth to the wind when it passes. The very presence of the boy changed the place. His songs left something up there.

He goes by another first name now. When asked, he tells a simple story: He fell, he slept, he was scared; he survived because of a rucksack of snacks.

He knows people were cheated of the story they expected. Or wanted. He knows that when he was found alive he became a walking reprimand.

The posters and leaflets were recycled, the police went away, the liaison officer got promoted, Robert and Jolie's marriage disintegrated, Peter Blythe stopped showing new work. Lanny is taller and hairier now, he moves more slowly, asks fewer questions and thinks straighter about man and nature. He huddles behind the bus shelter smoking and laughing with his friends.

He has tried to lose the memory of Dead Papa Toothwort. Like the last speaker of any language he has had to forget in order to survive, but some knowledge of it lives in his marrow.

I could go on, but watch:

Deep in a silvicultured English wood there's an old man sitting on a stump gazing at the roots of a fallen tree.

He gets out a big pad of paper and two wooden boards.

He opens a little box of charcoal and removes a fragile stick of burnt willow. He sits and does nothing but look for ten minutes. The beech trees watch him, safe under their canopy.

Then he starts by moving across the page with just the dry heel of his hand, not making a mark, just letting his arm and his eye and the forms he's looking at become acquainted, and then in confident strokes he starts to draw the roots, starts to let them take shape on the page. His line leaps and pesters at the idea of the roots, and the roots play at being bones, tangled bodies, burnt buildings, ravaged metal frames of industrial leviathans, profiles, serpents, knots and cavities, and he smiles because as he darkens and works them they start looking and feeling like tree roots.

'Mad Pete.'

'Ah, good evening sir.'

The old man bends and drops his drawing on the floor. He stands, clutching a hand to his lower back, to the pain in his bones.

'Come here then.'

The two men embrace. The younger man is a foot taller and he smiles as he stoops into the hug, seeing the drawing on the floor.

'Nice.'

'All right, Master Dürer, you have a go.'

The young man takes two bottles of beer from his rucksack. He digs about to find his keys then pops the lid off both and offers one to the old man. They chink and drink.

'This is from Mum,' says the boy, handing the man a book. 'A signed copy of her latest.'

'Oh bloody hell, more nightmares.'

'Always more nightmares.'

The old man rips a sheet from his pad and secures it with a metal clip to the spare board. He hands the board and a stick of charcoal to his companion and nods at the upturned tree.

They have an hour or two of good light left.

They draw the woods around them.

Love and thanks:

Lisa Baker.

Mitzi Angel and Ethan Nosowsky.

All at Faber, Graywolf, Aitken Alexander and Granta.

Kate Ward, Louisa Joyner, Eleanor Rees, Jonny Pelham, Rachel Alexander, Kate Burton, Catherine Daly and Katie Hall.

Lucy Dickens.

International publishers, translators and friends.

Most of all, for everything, thank you Jess.

GRIEF IS THE THING WITH FEATHERS

Winner of the International Dylan Thomas Prize and shortlisted for the Goldsmiths Prize and the *Guardian* First Book Award

In a London flat, two young boys face the unbearable sadness of their mother's sudden death. Their father, a Ted Hughes scholar and scruffy romantic, imagines a future of well-meaning visitors and emptiness.

In this moment of despair they are visited by Crow – antagonist, trickster, healer, babysitter. This sentimental bird is drawn to the grieving family and threatens to stay until they no longer need him.

'Amazing and unforgettable.' *The Times*

'Unlike anything I've read before.' Andrew McMillan, *Guardian* Books of the Year

'One of the most surprising books this year.' *Spectator* Books of the Year

'Dazzlingly good.' Robert MacFarlane

'A luminous reading experience.' *TLS*

'Utterly astonishing. Truly, truly remarkable.' Nathan Filer, author of *The Shock of the Fall*

www.faber.co.uk

ff